Praise for Angela Slatter

'Angela Slatter is a powerful and eloquent voice in horror fiction. Every story in this collection is a dark and polished gem.' ~ **Stephen Jones**

'Angela Slatter is one of the treasures of current horror fiction. Her work is darkly magical, lyrical, and beautiful, and I can't recommend it highly enough.' ~ **Alison Littlewood**, author of *A Cold Season, The Unquiet House, A Cold Silence, The Path of Needles*

'Marvellous stuff! Angela Slatter confronts the darker side of humanity in these bracing meditations on the nature of belief, betrayal, and wonder. *Winter Children and Other Chilling Tales* is a riveting read, and a fine addition to the canon of one of the genre's fastest-rising stars.' ~ **Helen Marshall**, author of *Hair Side, Flesh Side* and *Gifts for the One Who Comes After*

'Angela Slatter's stories are enviably original, and told in prose as stylish as it's precise. Not just disturbing but often touching, her work enriches and revives the tale of terror.' ~

Ramsey Campbell, author of *The Doll Who Ate His Mother*, *The Hungry Moon*, and *Told by the Dead*

'Angela Slatter is an international treasure. She blends horror, fantasy, and fairy tale to create something entirely fresh, but which feels too like the nightmares half-forgotten when you were a child.' ~ **Robert Shearman**, author of *Love Songs for the Shy and Cynical*, *Remember Why You Fear Me*, and *They Do the Same Things Different There*

'Angela Slatter's wonderful collection is filled with tales of gruelling horror and shiver-inducing dread, often swathed in shades of the darkest humour. You won't want it to end.' ~ **Tim Lebbon**, author of *The Silence* and *The Hunt*

WINTER CHILDREN AND OTHER CHILLING TALES

ANGELA SLATTER

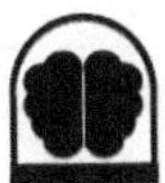

Brain Jar Press
PO Box 6687
Upper Mt Gravatt, QLD, 4122
Australia
www.BrainJarPress.com

Cover design by Peter Ball
Cover Image: Tithi Luadthong/Shutterstock

ISBN: 978-1-922479-01-3

Contents

Thank you:

To my wonderful family.

To the lovely folk at PS Publishing for the original limited edition version, and to the equally lovely folk at Brain Jar Press for the paperback and ebook versions.

To the readers who love a taste of darkness in their bedtime reading, to the editors who loved these stories, and to the beta readers who helped along the way (you know who you are).

To the Katharine Susannah Prichard Writers Centre for the time and place to complete the edits, and to the Copyright Agency for assistance with funding

Only the Dead and the Moonstruck

BECKY HEARD the clink of the beer as he tried to slide it silently out of the fridge.

'Put it back,' she said, 'or I'll tell Mama.'

Micah swore almost under his breath, but loud enough for her to hear what he thought of his little sister. The bottle made an angry sound as he replaced it. Then there was the soft thud of the juice bottle and the little fermented sigh as he uncapped it that told her it was almost out of date. She knew without looking that he was drinking straight from the carton; it was the kind of thing he did nowadays. She heard him slip back onto his chair and start hacking at the fried chicken on his plate. On her lap, Riddle, the fat ginger cat, stirred and sniffed, settled again, knowing that no food escaped the boy.

She tuned out the noises of her brother's meal and watched her mother, as she always did, through the sunflower gauze curtain. Becky wasn't sure if Suellan knew she was there, but she thought not; the woman was too focused on the sky. The stars were bright the night Aidan, Becky's eldest brother, had disappeared, and Suellan by her own admission couldn't help herself, not even two years down the track. Not even a new town, new house, new life could stop her from going onto the narrow porch, a glass of red in hand, after she'd served up their dinner (always late, always around nine) and taken a few bites of her own, to stare upwards, judging the quality of starlight, hoping that one night they'd shine bright enough for her boy to find his way home.

And Becky understood. She understood a lot of things: that her mother hadn't believed the police when they'd said Aidan had run away, nor when they changed their story to *abducted*. That Suellan sure as hell hadn't believed them when they'd tried to tell her that the decomposed body lying on the steel tray at the Arkham morgue was all that was left of her son after he'd finally been found in the river. After all, she'd said to Becky's father Buck, there was really only the right forearm with enough pale puffy skin left to show the places where it seemed something had suckled and bit with all those tiny ring-a-ring-a-roses of sharp teeth, and that could have belonged to anyone.

It didn't matter that the ragged clothes wrapped around the rotted form were identical to Aidan's. Didn't matter what they told her about DNA. Didn't matter when they said Aidan wasn't the first Essex County boy to whom this had happened. Didn't matter that she'd eventually given in to Buck's pleas that they move, start again. Becky remembered her father asking, *Didn't the other kids deserve a future that wasn't overshadowed by their brother's passing?* But she couldn't recall her mother answering.

Didn't matter, Suellan told Becky and Micah more than once, coz one day their big brother was coming back and he'd know where to find them because of the starlight, because it would lead him home. To her.

'You got homework?' Becky asked Micah and received a

grunt, which she interpreted as *Yes*, and said, 'Leave it on my desk.'

In Suellan's memory, Aidan was fifteen forever, unchanging and perfect, filled with potential and always *just* on the cusp of returning; she had hung onto that idea, but Becky could see what it did to Buck. He'd given up, in the end; she and Micah had come home from school one day and he told them. Wanted them to understand he couldn't bear it any longer, couldn't bear Suellan, how she'd brought everything with her: the sadness, the baggage, the hurt, everything they'd needed to jettison if they were to become light enough to keep living. He said things like that sometimes, poetic things, pretty things, useless things. Buck had taken just two suitcases, and the new house was as cluttered as the old with golf clubs, wetsuits, tennis rackets, the spear gun Suellan had given him one birthday so he could take the kids floundering. So many discarded things spilling from the garage and into the laundry, taking up corners and shelves, because Buck's wife couldn't be bothered to get rid of it all even after he left.

Suellan had continued to function, though, and Becky was grateful for that, grateful that her mother could hold down the freelance copywriting jobs and work from home, get paid a good wage, with a health care plan and all. She looked after her remaining offspring, and Becky knew she tried hard not to punish them for being Buck's kids, or for not being Aidan.

'Any more chicken?' asked Micah, surprisingly articulate when he wanted something. Becky, having eaten two packets of Red Vines after school, wasn't hungry. The cat began to purr, a low thrum that sent gentle vibrations through her knees.

She shrugged, didn't take her eyes off Suellan's thin shoulders and narrow back. 'Have mine.'

Adolescence had changed Micah in a way it hadn't for

Aidan, making him a surly, slouching, testosterone-scented troglodyte. But Becky, with love and guilt—so much guilt!—reminded herself every day to cut him some slack. They'd both suffered from the loss of Aidan, but Micah had taken Buck's desertion especially hard. He wore t-shirts and jeans that had belonged to his brother. Sometimes their mother's eyes caught on a shirt, recognition sparked and so did a tear, but she didn't say anything, just watched Micah as if she imagined he was her lost child.

Becky wondered if the terrifying transformation that had taken Micah would affect her too. She had a year before she became a teen, and she watched the time pass with a kind of resigned fascination. Maybe there wasn't anything she could do about it.

'Can you hear that?' Micah asked, words pushed out around masticated chicken and crumbed crust. Becky didn't turn, just tilted her head and listened carefully.

'Nope. You're hearing things. Did you leave the TV on?'

He didn't dignify that with a response; the television was always switched off as soon as dinner was on the table. Becky didn't get resentful like others might; she was a good student, a good daughter, a good sister. She was patient with her mother and brother, and accepted her self-imposed burdens and duties, and she did it a lot out of love, but even more out of guilt.

Because Becky had seen the girl and told no one.

From her bedroom window she'd watched Aidan leave the house and wander down the path that starry night. Seen the dim shape of someone waiting outside their fence, where the porch light was weakest, where the gloom hid the sloping bank and the river that was sometimes sweet, sometimes salty coz it ran out to the sea not so far away. Seen it resolve itself into a strange-looking girl who drifted back and forth, as though she swam through the air. Becky almost called out, but then saw her brother lift a hand to the visitor. She couldn't see his face, but she thought he was wearing that shy smile he had, and went straight to the girl's arms and snuggled right into her as if it was the place he most wanted to be. It was then Becky realised what had drawn her to the window in the first place was the girl's song, guttural, like one frog calling to another.

And that girl with skin as pale as a fish's belly, thick lips, and wide-set protruding eyes that even in the moonlight appeared to have no whites, had looked up at Becky's window. That girl seemed to see her, even in the darkness, even through the lacy curtain. And that girl smiled slowly to let all those tiny teeth catch the rays of the moon and stars.

And Becky had peed her pants.

And Aidan hadn't come home.

And Becky had never told.

She'd never told because inside her head she'd heard the girl's voice, her words all wet and throaty and slow. Words that numbed Becky's mind until everything the girl said was reasonable, a seed planted that kept the younger girl's mouth shut forever afterwards, because Becky knew she'd made a bargain and if she broke it she would lose even more than she already had. So, she let Aidan go and was grateful to have kept Micah.

Behind her there was a burp, deep and long, the kind produced only by the stomach of a teenage boy. The kind that penetrated the double-glazing and made Suellan startle and shiver. Becky shook her head and threw Micah a withering glance. He shrugged and stood, leaving his plate where it was. That was okay: it was her week to stack the dishwasher. He took the distance to the living room in two long strides.

'Don't forget your homework,' she called after him, but the only answer was the thud of his overly large sneakers on the carpeted stairs. She listened, tracking him along the corridor, into his room, out again, to hers, door thrown back to hit the wall as always, then three steps to her desk. She imagined the harsh whisper of the school books hitting the cheap laminate, then Micah's footsteps as he retreated to the bedroom set up just as it had been when he'd shared with Aidan at the Arkham house. Bunk beds and the two desks cramping the much smaller space, walls covered by the same posters, shelves heavy with the same baseball mitts, interesting rocks, pieces of driftwood, and assorted sporting trophies. As if Micah was wrapped in an Aidan-cocoon. He'd be asleep soon; he slept so much, early and late.

'Frogs are going crazy out there,' said Suellan and slammed the kitchen door. Riddle, startled, dug his claws through Becky's skirt and into her thighs, but didn't bother to leap off. Becky bit back a curse and looked reproachfully at her mother. Suellan smiled, leaned down, and scratched her shocking-pink nails along the amber fur.

'Stupid cat,' she murmured, then switched her attention to Becky and ran her fingers through the girl's mouse-brown hair. Becky, like Riddle, closed her eyes for a few seconds, just that tight temporal sliver when everything was okay: the darkness behind her lids was warm and the hand upon her was gentle. For that tiny moment, there was comfort and things were all right. Then Suellan moved away and Becky heard the sound of her wine glass being set carefully on the bench, then the running of water into the tumbler her mother always took up to bed, to wash down the tranquillisers the doctor kept giving her. 'Night, Becky.'

'Night, Mama. Lots of stars tonight,' she said but got no response. When she opened her eyes Suellan was gone, moving silently as always on her long legs. Becky blinked, and couldn't remember the last time she'd felt a goodnight kiss on her forehead. She sighed and rose, dislodging the cat, who squeaked indignantly. 'Oh shush, hairbag.'

Riddle sat in front of the cat door, as if threatening to desert, but he'd never used that exit in his life, preferring to yowl until someone opened the people door for him, and he wasn't about to change habits now. He began to wash his ears, watching as she packed the dishwasher, which took more time than it should because they only ran it once a day. Becky didn't mind. It was quiet time for her to plan, to get her ducks in a row. She always did her homework as soon as she got home from school, so there would just be Micah's—it was Tuesday, so probably algebra and English.

She slotted the last coffee mug into place then put the soap tablet in the tiny box that was supposed to release as soon as she closed the dishwasher. Becky remained convinced it sometimes hung on for a while, freeing the thing only when it felt like it. Just like she was certain the fridge light stayed on that little bit longer, to assert some kind of independence. Straightening, she peered out the window into the shadowy garden.

Becky took in the colour of the night, how it changed the objects it touched: the swing set she hardly used anymore, the folding sun-chairs, the defiantly unhappy rosa rugosa bushes, the palings leeched silvery by salty air. Sand blew up from the shore and piled against the fence, crept through to make the lawn grainy. She looked beyond the yard, out to where the land fell away and a path led down through a thin barrier of shrubs and stunted trees until it met the beach proper. She stared and stared, lost focus, and fell into a kind of trance until something pale ran right past the pane, leaving a smear of afterimage on her surprised gaze.

Becky gasped and stumbled back, then leaned close again and scanned the empty scape. Something else moved further away, between the trees, paler still, glowing, and then it was gone. At the door there was the sound of the handle being tried, and Becky turned; she didn't know if Suellan had locked it when she came in. Becky always checked just before she headed upstairs, and sometimes it was locked, others not. The doorknob rotated, slowly at first, then faster as it became obvious that the latch held and whatever was attempting to get in was becoming increasingly frustrated.

She had only just begun to savour her relief when the square-cut flap at the bottom of the door was pushed open, and a greenish-grey hand with long nails and webbing between its fingers darted in, found Riddle's fat rump and dragged the surprised animal out before he managed even a squeak of protest.

As she reached out, her first instinct was to open the door, try to save the cat, but the cold part of her brain said *no*. It stayed her hand, and she backed away, spun on her heel, and ran up the stairs, past Suellan's door—experience had shown that her mother would be not be roused until the sun came through her window in the morning—into her own room. Becky crouched by the window, peering over the sill, trying to see where the thing was.

And there it stood, in the middle of the yard, head raised, flattish nostrils dilating as it drew in great lungfuls of sea breeze. Becky thought it—*she*—wore a dress, something long with sleeves, something bleached. In its—*her*—arms was the cat, who lay frozen as the talons brushed up and down his pelt. Only the gleam of moonlight in Riddle's eye told Becky how afraid he was.

The house was locked, thought Becky, they were safe.

It couldn't get in; everyone else was asleep.

There was just Riddle, poor old Riddle, and he was a goner.

Becky bid him a silent guilt-ridden goodbye, and slumped against the wall. In her heart she was affronted that the thing, the girl, had broken their bargain, that she'd come seeking again, but she knew she shouldn't have been shocked. Hadn't she spent all that time reading after Aidan had gone, researching in the library? Hadn't she seen a pattern?

Disappearances stretching back so far that those old microfiched newspapers called it 'the Harvest' or 'the Arkham Harvest'. Didn't she find over one hundred years of reports saying annually how baffled the police were? It didn't matter that they'd moved, because Kingsport wasn't so far from Arkham, as the crow flies—or the fish swims—and hadn't she'd found evidence of teenage boys vanishing not just here but across the length and breadth of Essex County? All the strange girl had to do was follow the path of starlight and the scent of Suellan's longing, to come up from the cold waters and trek along the beach until she reached their front door. All she'd had to do was wait, bide her time until Micah had ripened, until he was giving off those odours and hormones that said he was fresh meat.

But the house was secure and Micah was asleep, wrapped in that heavy unbreakable teenage-boy sleep that rivalled Suellan's drugged slumber. Becky just had to wait. Sacrifice the poor old cat and wait for the dawn, figure a solution tomorrow when the sunlight burned away terrors. The rush of adrenaline began to wear off, and in its place came the sluggish flow of exhaustion. It crept through her limbs and she closed her eyes. She sat there in front of the window so long that she began to drowse, head drooping; from somewhere a song seemed to start, at first lulling her, numbing her mind, calming her until she had almost slipped to the bottom of night's well ... but then she realised that the beat was wrong. It wasn't a lullaby, or a comfort; it was familiar and the memory of it made her shudder and fight, swim up from the darkness and awaken.

The girl had begun, at some point, to sing: a siren song of amphibian longing, a soothing, a calling, a summoning, so low at first that Becky barely heard it. But it had gotten louder, triumphant, and then Becky had recognised it. She wondered if Aidan had fought or simply given in because it was easier than anything else, because the tune had convinced him to go quietly as easily as it had convinced her to let him go.

Then she heard, quite distinctly, the slap of large bare feet on the linoleum downstairs, the kitchen door being unlocked and thrown open to bang against the wall. She struggled up as if swimming in glue and stared down through the glass, watched as the girl's smile widened and she opened her arms to the boy covered only by his ratty boxers. Riddle, released, sped back into the house, a streak of frantic flame, passing Micah as he padded into the yard.

It was only when they'd trudged off into the gloom that Becky found she could move freely again. She took the stairs so fast she almost fell, yelling without hope that Suellan would wake. Sprawling into the kitchen, she hauled open the cutlery drawer, looking through the knives, rejecting each one because none seemed big enough for the task at hand. Then, as she sobbed, she remembered all Buck's abandoned things, the remnants of him that haunted the house: the golf clubs, the tennis rackets. The spear gun waiting atop the laundry cupboard, where Suellan had stashed it when Becky was smaller and unable to reach, but now … She'd grown just enough that she could jump and tap the handle visible at the edge, just enough to dislodge it; one more jump and it dropped, followed by one—only one!—of the spears. But she didn't have time to climb up and see if there was another; she had to get out, out, following her brother and the girl. Becky slid that precious bolt into place, just as her father had shown her.

Outside, the clouds had covered the moon and the stars had dimmed, so she ran in the direction they'd disappeared, guided only by the textures under her bare feet: grass soft then gritty; then small stones, some sharp, some smooth; then coarse sand as she found the path; and finally the shingle itself with all the fine loose particles that made movement so difficult. And it was dark, so very dark, and she couldn't make out anything in that blackness as she hefted the weight of the gun and felt … not the trigger, but the button, the button of the light that Buck had fitted to the weapon. She remembered how proud he'd been when he got it to work. Becky pressed the switch and a weak yellow light leaked. She swept the pitiful circle ahead of her, across the beach until she found them in a huddle halfway to the water, as if the girl couldn't wait.

Micah was draped across her knee and left arm; her right steadied his shoulder, while her head bowed over his chest. Sensing the pale wash of light, the girl lifted her face and Becky saw how full of teeth her mouth was. And her tongue, her long tongue, the tip of it suckered lamprey-like to the boy's bare torso. Becky screamed and the girl hissed, dropping Micah to the sand and standing, arms at her sides, the batwing sleeves of the dress spread.

Becky fired. She had the girl dead to rights and the barb flew straight, but at the last moment she shifted like an eel and the spear went through the wing of her sleeve … no, not a sleeve, Becky realised.

Webbing.

The webbed skin tore and the girl shrieked, flapping the left arm against her side in pain, making the wet hole bigger, bigger. Becky took her gaze from the girl, just for a second, to see if Micah was moving, but she couldn't tell. Then the girl, the thing, moved faster than Becky would have thought possible and rushed towards her, the uninjured arm striking out and connecting with Becky's jaw. She saw starbursts against her eyelids, and she wished as hard as she could that she'd had more than one spear.

Becky dropped the gun and the light flickered off, and it didn't matter that she opened her eyes because clouds had rolled in and the night was pure pitch and all she knew was that the girl was looming above her, and then the breath *whumped* out of her as the creature settled on her chest. Then there came the oily sting of something attaching itself, snakelike, to her shoulder, between the neck and the collarbone, and Becky couldn't believe how much it hurt. She couldn't believe Micah hadn't been yelling and screaming when she'd found them, not with this happening to him. She wondered if the girl would just injure her badly, incapacitate her, then make her watch as Micah was taken; wait until her heart, already battered by the loss of Aidan, was broken completely, and only then kill her.

And Becky could feel something other than blood flowing from her: life and energy were drawn out, replaced by pure anguish because she knew she couldn't do anything to stop it.

Then, as despair settled on her, heavy as the girl herself, the clouds were caught by a new wind, and pulled apart. The moon and the stars were revealed in all their shocking brightness, lighting up the stage of sand and sea as if it was an open-air theatre, and the girl, her tongue releasing Becky and falling limply away, froze.

Becky twisted, finding the girl easy to throw off. She half-scrambled, half-crawled towards Micah but, realising the beach was brighter than it should have been, she glanced around. A shape in the form of a young man drifted over the waves and the sand, untroubled by salty water or grit for he floated above both. As he drew closer, Becky recognised him, and whispered a silent apology for ever doubting her mother.

It was Aidan, drawn home, but Aidan remade, with starlight and moonlight running through him.

Aidan, but Aidan as if he wore light as a shroud.

Aidan, but Aidan as if his life, his death, his afterlife were transparent layers. Becky could see the skeleton innermost, then the pale muscle and flesh, then the punctured, suckled-upon skin holding all the marks to show how he'd died, and, finally, the astral radiance that wrapped him all round, and shone from his eyes and his mouth and his nose. His light began to pulse and pulse and pulse.

And the sight of him, oh! The sight of him made the girl, who'd taken his life so boldly, cower and shrink.

Becky smiled at her eldest brother but he didn't smile back, didn't seem to see her, just concentrated on the girl as the shining intensified and then blazed out surely as a solar flare, engulfing everything.

Becky was blinded for long moments. When she at last blinked away the searing whiteness, was able to focus and remember what had happened, she became aware of a scent: ozone and fried fish. Not far away she saw Micah, sitting up as if waking, rubbing his head. She struggled over, hugged him until he laughed and told her to stop. And they found they were both crying.

'What happened?' he asked and she didn't know how to explain.

Then she realised that the beach was still lit, though moon and stars were once again hidden by clouds. She turned and found Aidan, hanging in the air a few feet from them. She wondered if he would fade, disappear, his work done, his siblings saved. But though they stared for a long minute, then another, then another and another, their brother, transparent and luminescent, remained in place.

Becky didn't know what was worse: having sacrificed him, or having him back. The remorse that made its home inside her welled up and stuck in her throat. Did he know? Did Aidan know what she'd done? What was he, now? Swallowing, she made a decision and with halting steps, Becky approached. She reached out and took Aidan's hand, which was as fragile and airy, as cold and sharp, as she imagined starlight to be. She tugged at him and he floated along beside her. Micah stood, watching, waiting, afraid to touch.

'What do we do?' he asked and Becky shrugged.

'Tell Mama she was right.'

Cuckoo

THE CHILD WAS dead by the time I found her, but she suited my purposes perfectly.

Tiny delicate skin suit, meat sack, air thief.

The flesh was still warm, which is best—too hard to shrug on something in full rigour—and I crammed my bulk into the small body much as one might climb into a box or trunk to hide. A fold here, a dislocation there, a twinge of discomfort and curses when something tore, stretched just too far.

The rent was in the webbing of the right hand. Only a little rip, no matter. The sinister *manus* was my favoured choice of weapon anyway. I sat up, rolled my new shoulders —gently, carefully—then stood, rocking back slightly on legs too tender, too young to support my leviathan weight. I took a step, felt the world tilt, caught my balance before I fell and risked another tear; looked down at the single pink shoe, with its bows and glitter detail; took in the strange white cat face that ran around the hem of the pink and white dress; rubbed my miniature fingers against the dried brown stains that blotched the insides of my thighs.

The child had died hard.

The sliver of me that retained empathy ached, just a bit. But I could smell the scent of the one who'd done this and I would follow that scent. The hunt was on, my blood was up. Time was of the essence—my presence will speed decay. I pitched my head up so my nostrils caught the evening breeze and breathed deeply, filling my borrowed lungs, so the memory would remain.

Again, I took a step, more, all steady.

Determined. Forward.

HERE'S THE THING: evil used to be different.

It used to be black and white. It used to be more *obvious*. Nowadays? Everyone on this planet is tainted to some degree. Once upon a time, there were villains of a memorable —perhaps even admirable—scale. But now?

Without contrast it's hard to see the differences.

I miss that—the delineation of great evil from banal nastiness.

I'd walked for two hours and the girl's legs were sore. I sighed and stepped into his front garden with its fastidiously dug flowerbeds planted with purple-red and saffron blossoms. The house was neat and tidy, a thin building running the length of the block, rather than across—I didn't need eyes to tell me that, just the child's memories. I dug around in her fading box of remembrances and found the floor plan of the house, vague as if seen in a rush. Hallway, all the doors to the left: a living room, then two more rooms, then a kitchen at the very back where he'd taken her for a glass of water. A staircase near the front door leading up: two bedrooms at the front and a bathroom at the back. The second bedroom she remembered most.

The walls had a shimmer to them and dancing fairies

were stencilled around the baseboards and just beneath the architraves. The bed was covered in a Barbie-branded duvet and so many frilly purple cushions they seemed like an eruption of fabric mumps. Shelves ran across two of the walls, burdened with My Little Ponies in every hue and style, too high for a child to reach.

And the cupboard, painted pink so it appeared as a mouth in a white face. And inside the cupboard, all those shoes, all those single left shoes, tossed in like so much refuse, as if the fetish could never be tidy. As if the inner workings would always be *messy*. Somewhere in that pile, maybe balancing precariously on the top, maybe toppled down the back, was the shoe he'd taken as she sat on the bed, before he did *anything*.

The mind began to shut down, the memories becoming the blurred white-blue of blind eyes. I clenched a hand, heard the joints crack. Time was running short.

I didn't need long.

A knock on the door, harder than intended, hurt my knuckles. I heard him moving around inside. I coiled inside the body, bracing myself against the slow wash of congealing blood and decaying organs, against the sea of human soup the child was becoming, and prepared to spring the moment I saw what I needed.

He opened the door.

Mr Timmons gave me nothing. Nothing but a slow steady blink. His eyes shifted from the dark marks around the delicate throat, down past the bruised thighs, and lit on the bare foot.

No fear. No guilt. No remorse.

I felt sawn off at the knees. Robbed. At a loss.

He twitched a sort of smile in my direction and slowly closed the door once more.

And I didn't do a thing.

I, who once commanded legions, who fell through fire and rose again, who felt the earth shudder beneath my feet, who took into me the souls of the greatest of the worst, I … did nothing.

THE WOMAN WAS in the wrong place at the wrong time.

But then, aren't they all?

I'd lain quiet for ages in the alley, just the bare foot sticking out to get attention. About four in the morning, she staggered along in her high heels, saw the pale flash of flesh and stumbled over to kneel beside me. The woman leaned in and I grabbed her. I wrapped my arms around her neck and covered her mouth with one hand, pinching her nostrils shut with the fingers of the other. I held her that way until the life drained out and she released her last breath, emptying herself in a final humiliating gesture of humanity. It's easier when they're dead, they no longer have the will to fight; if you have to expend energy battling for a body, you're not in best shape for the contest to come. I stood over her and let the child's form go, unpicked myself from the rapidly putrefying corpse, then watched as it hit the asphalt heavily. It made a wet noise as the side of the face gave way on impact and the belly burst like an overripe melon.

I stayed outside for a few moments, stretching, feeling the night on what passes for my skin, just for a few moments, then did my contortionist's act and plunged into the woman. Roomier, to be sure, broad across the hips, fleshy thighs, the strange weight of breasts hanging at the chest—I cupped them, jiggled them about, found nothing to justify the fascination with them. Then I felt the fizz and buzz of alcohol in the veins, the unsteadiness of the legs, the jelly of the knees and that ache in the lower back from being pushed at the wrong angle by the height of the shoes.

I'm sorry, I said to no one in particular. I don't even know if I was. It'd been a long time since I'd expressed sentiment to anyone—anything beyond disgust and a sort of righteous boredom. I said it again, just to hear my voice, *I'm sorry. I need*

. . .

But I didn't continue. Didn't finish. Had neither necessity nor desire to offer explanations to the dead.

I SAT NEXT to him on the park bench.

He was feeding the birds, watching all the little girls on the jungle gym, nodding, friendly, to their mothers and nannies. He didn't notice me. At least, not until his nose began to twitch. An unwashed body will garner attention sooner rather than later. His head swivelled and his eyes took me in—not that I would have been of any interest to him. He smiled and pointed towards the children as they played.

'Which one's yours?' he asked, although he must have known, couldn't have thought for a moment that my shell, still in its nightclub finery with smudged makeup and bird's-nest hair, had care of any child. He grinned slyly, as if we were in cahoots.

I turned towards him, shifted my torso, the body beginning to lose its flexibility. My clumsiness made it look as though I was showing him the woman's breasts, *presenting* them.

Disdain. Contempt. Amusement. All of these were in his face.

I raised my stolen hand and clicked its fingers. Sparks flew but didn't take. I did it again and there were flames—at first just at the tips, then they crept to engulf the hand, scorching the arm, catching quickly on the synthetic fabrics of the woman's outfit. It sped across the shoulders, split its forces and half-leapt downward, while the other continued upwards to set the bleach-blonde coif ablaze. I smiled at him from lips that curled and blackened and shrivelled back against teeth furred from no brushing.

I watched him long and hard, waiting, poised for that look, that hint, that signal.

For the light in his eyes that said he was afraid—because they're all afraid, in the end, and that's why I can take them —for the whimpering as he begged for his life.

His eyes remained dead, but for a lazy curiosity.

He stood and walked away as my body burned to a symphony of children's screams.

I FOLLOWED him all the next day, incorporeal.

Vengeance has been my path for so many years. Centuries. Aeons. It's all I've known, or all I remember. I have taken what was just, from men great and ordinary, their only commonality being they had stolen lives that did not belong to them. One life or thousands unjustly snuffed out will bring my kind like a hunting hound. I have seen them all learn fear, all tremble when faced with their crimes and beg for forgiveness, more time, another chance. But this man. . .

There was *nothing* great about this man. There was nothing special but his refusal to *fear*.

I ventured into his house, picked through his things while he went about his daily chores. Sat on the sad mountain of shoes in the closet and wracked my brain. I heard the phone ring and he let the answering machine get it. An official voice, tired, disinterested, left him a message, obviously used to no response, but duty-bound to follow through. I listened, then watched intently as he quite deliberately erased the recording, not bothering to take down the number or name the caller had left.

I thought I had my answer.

. . .

THE SMELL of antiseptic was sharp enough to sting.

Soft-soled shoes squeaking on waxed floors, clangs of metal trays and bedpans, trolleys banging through swinging doors, alarmed squeals from heart rate monitors as people died, the constant *blip* of the lesser machines, the *swoosh* of uniforms as staff hurried by.

And finally, a private room, a quiet space, oddly enough in shades of pink, a room meant for two patients but in which only one was in evidence. The bed was a striking piece of machinery, up-down-sideways buttons, the not-quite-white linen from too many washings, a curtain around it all, ostensibly for privacy, but really so no one is forced to watch someone dying.

The woman was younger than she appeared, but still older than I imagined. She looked, no matter her real age, like a crone. She was shrivelled, cannulas in both hands, tied to a battery of technology. A slit marred her throat with a tube poking through it, and a machine breathed for her. Her hair was wiry iron-grey, her face etched with lines, her eyelashes absent. Her mouth, which I imagine to have been often pursed with disapproval in life, hung slack. Saliva gathered in the deep furrows at the corner, some dried and flaking beneath the new layers of damp spittle.

I doubted she had much spirit left, no will to fight.

I touched fingers to her thin, thin chest and looked for a way in. Through the skin, through the very pores and I felt ... I felt almost as if I was being pulled down as much as I was entering in. She didn't fight me as her life limped away, rather she swam around like the dregs swirled in a coffee cup and I sensed myself ... contaminated.

But still, I sat the wizened carcass up, and carefully turned the machines off before I tore out probes and the sticky pads of plastic that connected us. No use causing a stir, sending a signal. It was going to be hard enough to walk the old bat out of the hospital.

I swung my blue-veined legs off the edge of the bed and gauged the distance to the door. One chunk at a time would suffice: bed to door, door to fire stairs, fire stairs to parking lot, parking lot to the end of the first block, first block to the second block, then his house halfway down that very street, not so far away.

The linoleum was cold beneath my feet.

THE HOUSE WAS DARK, but not as dark as inside the woman's head. Insistent thoughts of her son papered the walls of her memory. He was small, so small in there. So tender, so sweet, so *vulnerable*.

Ill. I felt ill.

I stood at the door to the main bedroom, watching the moonlight sheer through the curtains. I traced its trajectory to the bed. It was empty, the coverlet undisturbed. I backed away. The brittle bones in the feet seemed friable, liable to snap at any moment. The steps down the hallway, the thin tightly woven carpet, gave no comfort. The door to the princess room was ajar. I pushed it open. It did not creak as I slipped inside.

He lay flat, head thrown back, mouth open. Snores issued forth. The mountain of cushions had suffered an avalanche and I couldn't help but trip against them as I approached. Light streamed in, hitting the sequins and glitter on the scattered squares of overstuffed fabric, throwing beams around the walls.

I drew in my own weight until the body was as light as a bird's bones and I crawled onto the bed. My movements caused no ripple. I knelt on his chest and began to gradually let the weight loose.

His breathing became irregular; he started to struggle and soon enough he opened his eyes. Blinked to try and make out the face that hovered above his in the moonlit dark. His lids peeled back, widened in astonishment. I leaned forward, hungering for that look, that hint . . .

His right hand wrapped around the old woman's ankle. I glanced down as his fingers caressed the cool, corrugated flesh, tracing the ridges of ancient veins, moving upwards.

I fled. I shot out of every aperture I could find and pressed myself against the ceiling as the barely-alive body slumped onto Mr Timmons. His hand did not stop moving.

I did not cling there long. I flew through the window and fell, tumbling, to the garden beds, pressed the dirt rough against my skin, breathed deeply the fertiliser's acrid perfume. All of this felt clean compared to the contagion that seemed to still coat to me.

I stood, shaking, and slid into the clean black of night.

The Burning Circus

SEMIRAMIS HASN'T BEEN to the circus in such a long time.

Other circuses, yes. *The* circus, no.

Above the stand of trees, over to the left where the road curves around to encircle the big park, the striped canvas of the Big Top can be seen, the flame-red pennants waving in the breeze. While she's pinning her eyes there as though it might disappear if not watched, she's not paying attention to her feet, and she stumbles, trips, does a kind of progressive dance but doesn't fall. The heel of her right Mary Jane, though, gives up the ghost—the shoes were old before she got them—and she tries to hammer it back to the sole with nothing but her calloused hands. About as effective as using spit for glue. She surrenders, and sets off once again, her gait now the strange staccato roll of a woman with unequal leg lengths.

When she goes up on the left foot it feels, just a little, like flying. Just a little like the old days, that sense of ascending without a tether, then the downswing onto the right, down further than you know you should go, just like that too. Just like wondering if someone was going to catch you. Semiramis knows now only she can catch herself.

The outside still makes her nervous, even though the breeze feels like a kiss. All that space, no confines. *Silly*, she thinks; it wasn't always thus. Only she'd gotten so used to being inside, so used to the sight of walls and an entrance that didn't open, not in such a long time. And that window, so tiny and up so high, with the bars, up too high for her to see if he was coming; she wondered some days if that was why he didn't come, coz she wasn't able to look out for him. But the sun arrived regularly, spearing in to wake her each morning—sometimes the rain too. After the first few years, after she got to know every inch of the walls, the ceiling, the floor, she started living inside her skull, only surfacing when they pushed food in through the trap at the bottom of the metal portal. Sometimes not even then.

But then one day, oh one day, the door *opened*—the whole, entire, actual door. Pushed hard to break the rust on the hinges, and two men standing there looking embarrassed as if they'd discovered her crouching over the stinking hole in the corner. That was it. No fanfare, no shining light, no great revelation, just a couple of fat deputies staring at her like she was something they were surprised to find.

Truth be told, she didn't recognise them. Then again, she'd never been able to keep faces straight in her head from the time she walked into the sheriff's office. The only ones that stayed were from *before*. The folk she'd known and thought of as her family. And she remembered how the world looked each time she flew. She remembered the scenes from every time she let go mid-air and was ever so briefly weightless. Those were the things she remembered. The *before* things.

'Semiramis Baxter?' One of them asked, his voice weak to match his chin. She paused. Recalled. Yes. Someone had called her that once. Someone had breathed it in her ear like it was the most precious thing to cross his lips. Yes, that was her.

As she walks, she says it, says her own name, just to hear it hang in the air, just to know it's real. That she's real and so is this, *this* freedom. This terrifying freedom to do whatever she wants.

'Semiramis Baxter, you've served your time.' But she didn't think she had. Because there hadn't been a trial, she was very sure; there hadn't been anything. Just talking to a man with a big hat and a star pinned to his shirt; talking to him and saying, 'I saw the one who did it, he had red hair, and a brown suit, a moustache and his teeth were all crooked.' And he nodded, nodded and called a grieving woman into the room, a woman who looked at Semiramis blankly but stared ever so hard at the brooch she wore. Stared and stared and stared. *Yes,* the woman said, *yes, that's the piece of jewellery my husband gave me.* And next there was a lock being turned. Turning on Semiramis Baxter and she vanished for such a very long time.

Then those men at the door, and her standing, trying hard to stretch her calves, her thighs, tripping in her haste to get to the exit, fearful that this offer of liberty, of *air*, would be rescinded. They handed her over to a nun, a penguin of a woman who seemed not to sweat, in spite of the heat. The nun took her to a chapter house outside of the town—what was the town called? All this time and she couldn't bring it to mind. The other sisters took care of her, gave her a bath, washed and cut her hair (turned white far too soon), gave her two dresses, neither new. Laundered myriad times till they were pale and thin, but she didn't care. They were hers. And the shoes, the battered, brown leather Mary Janes with the wobbly heels. An equally battered suitcase and some plain underwear, a cloche hat that hadn't really had a shape for long years before it came to her. They gave her some money, dry paper dollars and coppery coins. They took her to the station and put a note in her hand with the name and address of a woman in Chicago who was expecting her to come and be the help.

She thanked them and smiled and got on the bus. She woke from a dream of his face as he gave *her* the brooch. She heard him saying, 'I'll come get you, my honey, my little peach, my one special girl. Only do this little thing for me—I can't help you if I'm locked up, can I?' She wanted to say, 'If I *don't* do this little thing I won't need your help,' but she didn't. She was a good girl. She walked right into the sheriff's office, just like Gabe asked, told the man exactly what he told her to say, wearing that damned brooch, the one that she knew too late Gabe had pulled from the woman's collar while she'd hunched over her husband as he bled out. Semiramis should have known it all along, when she found that scrap of green silk stuck to the pin when she unclipped it to put it on.

She'd opened her eyes, stared through the dirty windows, out at the wheat fields and the silos for a while, then got off the bus well before Chicago.

She kept moving, making money when she needed, not fussy about how she did it. Moving, moving, moving, always moving. Looking for them, looking for the troupe to which she'd once belonged, looking for *him*. So many states, so many cities, so many tiny, tiny little townships. It was so easy to disappear in this land; even a circus could find places to hide. Even one as queer as the Burning Circus.

She found other things along the way, other people who could and did help. The kindness of strangers was the strangest thing she'd ever encountered. And in New Orleans there'd been a woman with soft lips, gentle hands, and dangerous knowledge—a woman who'd showed her tastes she hadn't even known she had. This was the one who suggested what Semiramis might need, how she might get the amends due to her. This woman was the one who'd conceived them, such small things, so simple, not at all voracious—just needing some blood now and then, a bitty bit of meat. The soft part of Semiramis' upper arms, the inner flesh, was scarred over many times. And they took in a little of her pain, a little of her bitterness, a little of her righteous need for an accounting, each time they fed.

Then, having given Semiramis what she'd come for, having handed her the weapon of her requirement, the woman begged her not to leave—but she did anyway. Semiramis had wandered, here and there, following old posters and rumours, stories and lies and wishes. And she spent so much time thinking about how the circus had fled. How not a one of them had come to see her. Not a one had warned her. Not a one had stepped up in her defence. They were happiest attracting just enough attention to entertain people and encourage them to part with their coin for it. But anything more than that? Anything that might make someone take a hard look at Gable Brandt? Gabe who was gold to them all, coz he brought the crowds.

Didn't matter to Gabe that he pulled down the largest income of them all. It didn't stop him supplementing his income with creative acquisition. *That* night wasn't the first time he'd followed some fool woman to a dark corner and scared the gems off her—although it was the first time he'd left a corpse behind—and it wouldn't have been the last, Semiramis was sure. So she sat in diners, listened to gossip, followed whispers of theft, sometimes asking questions but not too many.

Then one day, there it was—the poster. Not old either, not yellowed by wind and months past, not blurred by rain and sun. Not looking so worn that she knew she'd missed it. Them. Him.

This poster was *fresh*. And there they were, or some of them anyway: Timo the Dwarf, Lucia the Bearded Lady, Ferdi and Helenca the Siamese Twins, Veronese the Ring Master, Berto and Atla, the Lizard Woman, the singing bears, the deformed horse they passed off as a unicorn. Yet others she didn't know, new blood come along after she'd been left behind. And *him*, the finest-looking man she ever did see; oh, Gabe was older, she could tell, but he remained so muscular, his jaw so defined, his moustache waxed to such sharp points! Still the main act—the Lord of the Air.

She rounds the bend and walks to the ticket booth, pays out a few of her last coins, smiles at Billy J, whose voice was just breaking last time she saw him. Now he's a doughy-looking young man. He doesn't recognise her; no one would. She no longer resembles the bird-boned beauty with ebony hair and ruby lips, and she's heavier too—not so much physically, but the time inside, the enforced grounding, it's made her seem more affected by gravity.

Semiramis joins the flow of bodies heading towards the Big Top, her old suitcase, holes poked in the sides, thumping rhythmically against her legs. Sometimes it bumps other people but she ignores them, doesn't see their looks or hear their grumbling. She hears the noises from the case, though, and she hushes the creatures, tender as a mother. She's moving forward, forward, forward into the faded canvas palace, which smells of sawdust and sweat, grease paint and stale perfume. She finds a seat, planting herself determinedly at the end of the row and refusing to shuffle along; others must climb over her. She pushes her case beneath the seat and promptly forgets it. The show begins and she is riveted.

The older clowns are slower in their japes, less nimble than they were; the new ones have clever quick tricks and trips, pratfalls and practical jokes. Then the flea-bitten lions, and the tigers with toothache, their fur coming out in tufts every time they jump. Next the ill-tempered elephant, she recognises; its trainer is wary, someone she doesn't know. Jugglers, acrobats, the girl with the 'unicorn' are a passing, glittering parade.

Then there's Berto as he takes centre ring. Berto wearing his tiny shorts with all his hair waxed off so there's nothing for the fire to take hold of; his lack of eyebrows makes him look perpetually surprised. Every night, Semiramis remembers, he's rubbed down with a secret mix (the shorts, too, are soaked in it), the stuff that will burn, burn, burn without touching him. She can see how deeply the wrinkles have cut into his face, how dry his skin is after years of this treatment. *He's decrepit*, she thinks, and puts a hand to her cheeks as if for reassurance.

As she watches, Berto's wife Atla takes a lit brand, promenades about, showing it to the audience so they can all see it, hear the *crackle* as it swallows oxygen. Then Atla circles back and gently touches the torch to her husband, nightly living out many a woman's fantasy. And Berto, he goes up like a Roman candle, turning slowly in a circle, untouched by the flames, if not the heat. Semiramis looks away, examining the crowd, unnoticed; all *their* eyes are glued to the human torch as he makes a slow circuit of the ring, displaying himself like a saint proud of martyrdom.

Semiramis doesn't care.

They don't matter.

This isn't what she came for.

You might think Berto's what they all come to see, night after night, a man set alight, but no. *Now's* the time for the grand finale. Flying beats burning hands down.

As Berto's inferno dies down and Atla helps him shuffle

away, the Ring Master directs the spectators' attention upwards.

There *he* is, fine as fine can be, Gabe dressed in his long leotard, arms and chest bare. Even from here she can see the way his eyes sparkle, how they pass over the crowd, resting on all the pretty girls in their summer dresses, resting on their pearl necklaces and brooches, their bracelets and rings, assessing value and what he might get for them in the next town—and who might be the easiest mark. She wonders if he's killed anyone else in the time they've been apart, if any more heroic and unexpected husbands rounded corners as Gabe robbed a woman he thought was alone.

Beside him on the high platform is a girl, tiny, hollow-looking, staring at him like he's god, like he's life and death, and he is, with no net below. A man can burn on the ground to mild interest, but those who defy gravity? All the risk, all the glory. Oh yes, a catcher is gold. A flyer is replaceable as breath. That girl up there, as easy to substitute one for another as the sequins on her costume.

Semiramis remembers flying—the sensation of letting go, the moment before gravity realised you were hers, and then the strong hands at your wrists, the feeling that you'd defied everything and were still *alive*. All things have their time, though, she knows that now. All things, all scenes, all acts. No flyer stays aloft forever.

She imagines Gabe turning to flame, imagines the rope ladder disappearing in a twist of orange and red and gold. She imagines him up there, trying to get down fast enough to escape, leaving the girl behind in his haste. She imagines the burning debris falling, falling, falling onto all those pretty summer dresses, turning their wearers into so much pulled pork. She imagines him anointed with a crown of fire.

Semiramis shakes herself. These thoughts are pointless, weightless like so much expelled air. Beneath her seat, vibrating against the backs of her heels she can feel the suitcase, its contents reacting to her turmoil, linked to her as they are by blood, her tiny minions, her lovely light little demons. As inside, so it is without.

She finds she has lost time and realises that—if he hasn't changed the act—the girl's part is coming to an end. Gabe always was a creature of habit and he'd not do anything that distracted a gaze from himself. The girl flies towards him and he helps her up onto the platform, gestures vaguely to indicate the crowd should clap her efforts. Before the applause has died down, he launches into his finale, taking the attention as he executes a slow swing away from the platform, just as he always did in the old days.

How many? wonders Semiramis. *How many between this girl and me? How many did he fail to catch? How many got too spooked and ran? How many got left behind? How many, how many?*

He waits for the swinging to stop, for the bar to steady and become static. Then Gabe performs his masterstrokes, all his movements effortless. A casual clowning that has the audience laughing and gasping; he is an aerial drunk, standing, swaying, falling, catching himself at the last moment, looping himself gracefully back around the bar, refusing gravity's demands. He dances, grandstands, feints, makes the hearts below seem to consolidate into one organ, beating in time, pounding and swooping and diving in time with his death-defying acts. Oh, Gabe is worth the money all right.

And Gabe, oh Gabe never falls. Semiramis believes this implicitly, because this is what Gabe taught her. In all their time together, he never once even slipped. He never once used a net. *His concentration,* he'd told her, *was absolute.* It might look like he's mugging for the watchers below, but no, that's just part of the trick. Up there nothing can distract him. Not one thing. Never. Gabe has absolute faith that he will never fall.

Semiramis pulls the suitcase out from under her seat.

She places it on her lap and sets her fingers on the tarnished brash clasps. Hunching forward, she curls her body over the battered rectangle and sighs *Fly*. Two light touches, two whispered *snaps*, and she lifts the lid as she straightens.

The dirty-white, barely fleshed doves burst upwards, red eyes burning, wings flapping, flapping, flapping as they rise unerringly. Gabe is making his last turn, his final faux-forgetful misstep, hands reaching pretending to miss the bar, the ropes, everything. The birds catch him off guard, hitting him in the chest, the face, the eyes, unbalancing him, blinding him, defeating him utterly.

And he falls, he falls as surely as a duck shot out of the sky. He meets the ground with an astonishing sound, a sound Semiramis never thought to hear. All around her people scream and shout, cover their eyes, hold their children close as if they might protect them from the sight of poor old Gable with his bones all askew and his brain coming out his ears.

Semiramis ignores them.

They don't matter.

It was him she came to see.

Home and Hearth

CAROLINE HELD THE DOOR OPEN, listening to the keys make that gentle *clink-clank* as they hung from the lock. He pushed past her and she could smell the peculiar odour he gave off now: puberty and a state institution. As he crossed the threshold, his too-small shoes leaving mud on the new welcome mat (she'd thrown out the one exhorting a universal power to 'Bless this mess'), the house seemed to sigh.

Then again, maybe it was her, but she couldn't remember the air leaving her lungs.

Then again it might have been the heating system as it puffed out warmth.

'Coke?' she asked, following him down the long hallway. 'Or hot chocolate? Crisps? Marshmallows? I baked your favourite biscuits. They're not hot but I can warm them in the microwave. There's a cake too. Banana. Or—or—what would you like?'

She knew she was overcompensating, had schooled herself not to during the weeks and months, but he was back in the house not five minutes and already she was failing. She reached out and touched his face. It was a mistake. The feeling against her palm, the slight sweatiness, the burgeoning pimples beneath the skin, combined to make her shudder. She hoped he didn't notice.

'It's fine, Mum. I'm going to my room.'

Simon hadn't called her that in months, not since the trial started. Not since Geoffrey had his heart attack and told her as she sat by his hospital bed that he didn't think he could continue with, well, everything. Turning up at the court every day, dodging and weaving reporters and cameras, listening to their son's legal reps talk and excuse and obfuscate. It was all lies, he'd said. They both knew it.

She could have the house. And the money.

(*It's mine anyway*, she wanted to say, but didn't. *It always was*.)

He had to go, he'd said. For his *health*.

Then she had to tell their son what his father had decided —that he was *opting out* of the family. Men never like to clean up their own mess, she'd thought at the time as she watched a light go out in him. His answers had whittled themselves down to monosyllables. He stopped referring to his father. Stopped calling her 'Mum', or indeed anything but 'her.'

Ask *her*, he'd say to the barrister. Avoiding *her* gaze.

Caroline thought her eyes should probably be misty, a little heated with some kind of emotional response, but there was nothing. Oh well. Perhaps it would come later, when they got used to each other once more.

'Okay,' she said belatedly. He was already gone, disappeared up the stairs, closing the door. She walked into the sitting room, which was directly beneath his room, and listened.

A few steps as he walked from one wall to the next, stopped at the desk, the bookshelves, the wardrobe (she heard the creak of its hinges), then to his bed. She'd left his presents on the duvet, neatly stacked—he'd missed his thirteenth birthday in all the chaos. There was the *whump* as he sat down, then the double *thud* of his shoes hitting the floor. Then a steady series of noises as each carefully wrapped gift followed the footwear. Finally, silence.

She stood beneath him for a while, then turned to one of the front windows and tweaked back the edge of the long cream-coloured curtains. Through the wrought bars of the fence she couldn't see anything but cars parked in the street, the houses opposite, each like hers: tidy, fenced, tall, with manicured gardens, quietly comfortable. No one. No reporters. No yelling at the house, no trying to get into the yard, no knocking at the door, no flashbulbs blinding Caroline before she learned not to open it for them. In a deep, damned part of her soul she was grateful for the bombings that had made her son old news.

She took a deep breath and headed towards the kitchen.

THE FROZEN FOODS aisle seemed colder than usual. Or maybe it was the collection of eyes boring into her back that was giving Caroline the chills. She reached into the freezer and pulled out ice cream (vanilla), a chicken (medium), then packets of peas, beans, carrots, and chips. They all made a metallic sound as they hit the bottom of the trolley.

She'd left Simon sleeping; a note on the table gave him strict instructions not to leave the house and not to open the door to anyone. But she'd had to go out, had to stock up— two days home and he'd eaten most everything she had. That was what he did now: eat and play computer games in his room. Soon she would have to talk to him about school. He'd have to return to the world, but that was fraught with complications. They would have to move, she thought. A new house, a new town, a new life. Maybe she'd dye his hair, have it cut so he didn't look like the boy on the news reports. Mind you, if he kept eating this way, it wouldn't be an issue. Her son would disappear beneath layers of fat, cleverly camouflaged by his own body.

She couldn't think about all those details now, so she did what she could, which was to reach out and load up on cheeses, yoghurt, custard, and milk. As she turned, fighting the trolley's recalcitrant wheels, she looked up and saw them. The herd.

Twelve housewives, nearly identical: corduroy trousers in greens and browns, sharply pressed collared shirts under V-neck sweaters in various hues, with barely worn Barbour jackets and scarves hanging loose around necks that showed signs of wrinkling. Caroline knew them—she'd been one of them herself once.

It wasn't with hatred, precisely, that they were staring at her, nothing so strong, nothing so *moral*. It was just a kind of intense distaste: her dirty laundry had been aired very publicly. All the nasty domestic worms had poked their heads out of the shit-stirred soil of her home. They could look down on her ... but it was something more. She made them nervous. She'd been a carbon copy—her fall made them feel exposed, vulnerable. *There but for the grace of God go I*, and so on. Caroline's son had made them afraid of their own children.

Now, people stared at them and associated them with *her*. Their neat, tidy houses, highly financial husbands, overachieving children, all held up to scrutiny by the lower orders. Caroline almost smiled; then did. Waved and resisted the urge to walk up to them and chatter inanely about scone recipes or some-such. She knew she looked manic, the smile pinned to her lips, eyes fever-bright.

She made her way to the junk food aisle and began to stack brightly packaged carbohydrates and preservatives into the trolley. The more she bought now, she reasoned, the less often she'd have to come back.

At the checkout, the spotty teen ignored her for a while, grabbing items in a podgy hand with chewed nails and chipped pink polish and dragging them over the scanner, then tossing them behind where an equally spotty boy jammed the items into bags. Eggs beneath tins of ham and tomatoes, bread beneath frozen things. When the girl finally looked up to mumble the total, Caroline could almost see the cogs in the brain wake and haltingly turn; could almost hear the grinding. She watched as the bloodshot eyes widened and the lips trembled, the bottom one dropping open like a drawbridge on a slow timer. The girl stammered; she fumbled with Caroline's credit card, dropped the docket, stared and stared and stared.

The bag boy didn't look up.

As Caroline packed the food into the back of the Land Rover, she felt as if she was being watched. Expecting one of the mums brigade, she straightened and looked around.

A dishevelled figure stood motionless in the corner of the parking lot. Scuffed boots, thick trousers; bulked up by a couple of men's coats and a disreputable sweater, the figure removed its bright-pink beanie only when it met Caroline's eyes.

It was the woman. The other mother.

Caroline didn't—couldn't—budge. She and the Traveller watched each other forever until the woman shoved her hat back over the dark, tangled hair and shuffled off. The spell broken, Caroline could shift again, but her joints ached. It seemed every move she made hurt. Every bag she heaved was filled with wet sand.

It was a long time before her hands stopped shaking enough for her to put the keys in the ignition. She was dripping with sweat in the cold, cold car.

. . .

'MUM? MUM!'

Simon's voice in Caroline's ear and his hands on her shoulder shocked her awake. She'd been dreaming somewhere dark, somewhere the blackness was deathly thick.

'Mum!! Wake up!' He was yelling, her son. She could smell fear on him; it came off his skin in waves, mixed with the scent of adolescence. He stank.

Caroline recoiled, trying not to do so, managing to shuffle herself across the sheets without actually seeming to move. Her head felt full of cement. Only the sheer terror of having Simon's fingers anywhere near her had the power to shock her awake as surely as an icy bath.

She cursed herself for having taken a sleeping tablet—what was she thinking, making herself vulnerable?—but there were so many in the bathroom, hers, Geoffrey's, all the enthusiastically doled-out tranquilisers the doctor had heaped upon them early in the piece. And she hadn't slept properly in … She so needed to sleep.

And now her son had crept into her room and gotten close enough to touch her with hands that had—

'Mum, there's someone downstairs.'

'What's the time?' She struggled into a sitting position and squinted at the shining digital face on her bedside table. She could hear someone battering at the front door. It was 2:00 a.m. Surely not reporters. Surely not at this hour. Nor the police—double jeopardy and all, and he hadn't been out of the house since he'd been given back to her. He couldn't have done anything else, not yet.

Simon's face was white, his eyes huge. *My child is afraid,* she thought, admonished. His blond hair stuck up at all angles; coupled with his terrified stare, it made him look very, very young.

Caroline felt a deep stab of shame. He needed his mum.

She wrapped a thick chenille dressing gown around herself and tied it tight.

She crept along the hallway, past the grandfather clock with its regular rhythmic *tick-tock*, and down the stairs, Simon behind her, his hands holding onto the train of her gown just like he did when little and she was in the kitchen making his buttery toast. Back when he couldn't bear to be parted from her.

The door was shuddering and shaking under the force of the blows—she thought she could see periodic slivers of the world outside as the wood warped inwards with each hit. She wondered if the leadlight panels would break, but they seemed to bend and curve like rubber. She opened the hall cupboard and pulled out a cricket bat—Simon's when he was eight. It wasn't huge but it was hefty and she'd get in a good swing, by God. Caroline pushed her son away so she could have space. As she took the last two steps forward there was one final *slam* and the door vibrated on its hinges, then all was still.

She flicked on the porch light, wrenching on the door handle and pulling at the same time.

Nothing. A pool of yellow light trickled down into the garden like something spilled, and beyond its reach there was the moonlight, giving everything a strange blue tint. The front yard was empty, as was the street beyond, and there was nowhere for anyone to hide. There weren't even any desperate reporters staked out in battered Vauxhalls, snoring or smoking or mainlining bad coffee from the all-night service station fifteen minutes away. The cars sparkled with the night's frost as if someone had scattered diamond chips over them.

Caroline stepped out, her feet cold. A few more paces and something stuck to the sole of her left foot. She bent down and picked it up, glanced briefly at the piece of faded photographic paper.

'What is it?' Simon's voice quavered from well back in the hallway, and she couldn't help, was devastated by, the wave of contempt that washed over her.

'Nothing. Just some rubbish.' She pocketed the photo before she turned and went inside. 'Hot chocolate?'

He surprised her by nodding, by choosing her company instead of retreating to his cave yet again. Instead of making her feel that she was alone in the house despite his presence.

The kitchen was bright and warm and for a while she could pretend everything was normal.

THE GROUND WAS hard-frosted and the grass crunched and crackled like broken glass beneath her boots. Far behind her were the house and its rear garden backing onto the common, the drunken fence and the squeaky gate that led out.

White mist hung in front of her face and she struggled to breathe in the cold air. Sweat ran its way down her spine. Caroline chided herself: she hadn't been to the gym in months; her thighs felt like jelly and she couldn't even manage a brisk walk without puffing. As she reached the top of the incline, she stopped, trying not to gasp for breath, and surveyed the land below.

A curious combination of painted wagons, battered four-wheel drives, and campervans were scattered in a loose configuration someone might mistake for a circle. In what passed for the centre was a fire pit, with smoke still rising from last night's embers. There was a bustle of activity: the Travellers were preparing to move on. This was probably the longest they'd stayed in any one place, she thought, then tried to unthink the reason why.

She took a deep gulp of icy air that made her lungs burn in protest, and started down the slope.

It took them a while to notice her as they packed up like efficient little ants, but she stood at the edge of their campsite and eventually someone spotted her. Looked closer. Recognised her features. Nudged the person next to them. And so on.

Eventually they all gathered around, so many of them, but kept a few metres between her and them, as if she might be contaminated and *this* was judged the safe distance. Pinned beneath their collective gaze, Caroline felt *thin*—no, not just thin, but *starving*, soul-famished, as if nothing good had ever come from or gone into her.

The men looked at her hard, although some seemed to pity her, but the women ... the women *judged*. They peered at her as if they knew what she suspected, that somehow her son's rot had started with her, begun in the womb and come to fruition months and months ago. She felt as if she were a specimen, an experiment that had gone horribly, openly wrong. Just when she thought she couldn't take any more and was about to turn tail and run, the crowd parted, split by a knife of a woman.

Caroline opened her mouth but no words came. Instead she stood there for the longest time, lips parted, tongue wetly visible but mute. Then the other nodded and turned, gliding through the press of bodies. Caroline followed and the Travellers shifted, maintaining the safe corridor as she passed between them.

Without the layers of clothes, she was tall and thin. Her hair, pulled into a black plait, hung down below the waist of a long green skirt. As she walked, Caroline could hear bells and she remembered from all the days of the trial that the Traveller was weighted down with jewellery: bracelets, earrings, necklaces, anklets; her fingers were swollen with rings, silver, gold, with stones of every colour. She led Caroline to one of the painted wagons, up the wooden steps of faded red and into a warm, dark, musty space. The door closed behind them without either of them drawing it shut.

The space stretched forward but seemed smaller than it should have, a dim tunnel stuffed with boxes and books and stray items of clothing. The built-in bed was piled high with blankets and newspapers. An unlikely chaise longue took up space, lying on an angle as uncomfortable as a lizard in a too-small container. The walls were hung with paintings and tapestries, some things that looked like pages from illuminated manuscripts, pendants, misplaced wind chimes, strands of crystals, strings of dried garlic and flowers, and, in one instance, what looked like animal paws.

Caroline glanced away.

A pot of tea sat in the centre of a small table, neatly placed within the edges of an embroidered circle of birds and horses. Two cups. Like the teapot, they were once fine porcelain, now crackle-glazed, their floral pattern faded. Caroline thought her grandmother might have had the same set once upon a time. Her *hostess* sat and waved that she should do the same. Caroline hoped the woman—her name was Aishe, Caroline reminded herself—would speak first, but she knew it was her own place to do so. She, Caroline, even if not the sinner, bore the sins of her child.

Finding her throat closed, she put a hand in her coat pocket and pulled out the photo, laying it on the cloth between them.

Aishe ignored it, instead pouring tea. The liquorice aroma was strong, the liquid deepest black. Only when she had pushed the cup across the cloth to Caroline's side of the table did the woman let her gaze stray to the small, sad square of paper.

A little boy smiled up at them. He had black eyes and coal scuttle curls. His skin was olive and he wore a patched red sweater, worn cord trousers too large for him, and boots. He held the reins of a shaggy-looking pony and his joy was like a bolt of sunshine. Aishe's hand hovered over the snapshot, one finger lowered tantalisingly close to the boy's face, but at the last minute not touching it. She sat back, resigned, weary, and looked expectantly at her guest. Still she did not speak.

Caroline, never good with silence, scootched forward. She pushed the edges of the photo with the tips of her nails, as if to draw the woman's attention to it—to make her consider it more seriously.

'Yours,' she pushed out of her mouth. 'This is yours.'

Aishe shook her head, lids dropping heavily.

'Yes, it's *your son*.' Caroline's tone was sharp, a touch of desperation, a need to convince the other of what she was saying.

'No.' The word, when it rumbled out, showcased how deep her voice was. Caroline sat back. She couldn't recall ever hearing her speak, not during the whole of the trial. But surely ... surely she must have. The no-longer-mother had given evidence, hadn't she?

'No?' she asked.

'No,' repeated Aishe. 'Not mine. Not anymore.'

Caroline shook her head. 'I'm sorry. I'm sorry for what happened. I'm sorry for your son, but this photograph is yours. Please, please don't bother us again.'

'Drink. It will help.'

Against her will, Caroline did, sipping at the black brew.

'*Your* son,' said Aishe, 'has something inside him. Something wrong.'

'You think he's possessed?' Caroline scoffed. She'd been brought up in a home where religion was politely ignored except at Easter and Christmas, and she'd raised Simon the same way. Geoffrey was an atheist.

'So are all who do such things. The thing inside makes them so.' Aishe wrapped her hands around her own cup, ignoring its handle and drinking deeply.

'So ... so you say it's not Simon's fault?' As Caroline wondered at this offer of absolution, the other woman laughed.

'We still have a choice—free will. We always have the power to say yes or no. Your son has something inside him, yes, but he chose to give in to it.'

Caroline felt the words like a slap. She put the teacup down, her shaking hands clattered it on the saucer. She stood.

'I am sorry. Sorry about your son.' She made her way to the door, fumbled with the handle until it gave and let the cold sunlight in. She had her feet on the top step before she heard Aishe's last words.

'He's not *mine* anymore.'

Caroline stumbled but kept her balance. She tried to leave the rapidly shrinking laager with dignity, but the weight of eyes returning to her and the ringing of the woman's voice in her ears was a goad. In the end she ran. Ran out of the camp, up the hill, and then started down the other side, losing her footing and slipping and sliding on her arse to the bottom. She was up again in a second, running with a limp this time, tears freezing on her cheeks as she hurried towards the rickety gate and the drunken fence and what seemed like safety only in the vaguest of ways.

'Hello, Caroline.'

She'd made it to the entry to the back garden but found that she couldn't go in. Found that her hand wouldn't move to push the gate open, that her feet refused to turn. So, she'd kept going, wandered awhile, tried to lose herself in the woods. Stumbling through a stream that sluggishly dribbled along its wintery path, she'd fallen, torn the left knee of her trousers and the skin beneath. Eventually, she'd come out near the local shop and made her limping way home until her front door loomed large. Just as she pushed the wrought-iron front gate (unlike the back gate, the one in the front yard was respectable—it could be seen), that voice called softly from a car she hadn't recognised.

'Hello, Caroline,' he said again as he unfolded himself from the driver's seat.

Geoffrey was still tall, but he'd become very thin. And not been-to-the-gym-got-himself-in-shape thin either. Skeletal thin; not-eating thin; heartsick thin and it was almost enough to give her a little thrill of pleasure, to see he was still suffering.

'What the hell do you want?' She felt suddenly focused. The pain in her knee, which had been dull at best, burst into vibrant throbbing life. Anger flowed through her veins like molten silver. She was very much alert, alive, and she owed it all to the rage Geoffrey conjured in her.

He seemed to realise it and his steps faltered. 'I … I came to see you. And Simon.'

'I'm surprised you haven't let yourself in, made yourself at home,' she snarled, gloved hands clutching at the gate.

'You took my key away.'

She'd forgotten that. It had been the same day she'd taken his name off the joint accounts, and cut up his credit card. The same day she'd watched him stuff as many clothes as he could into a big bag on wheels and listened to it thump down the stairs. The same day he'd come home from the hospital and spent a grand total of forty-five minutes packing up the bits of his fifteen-year marriage he wanted to keep. He took no photos, no keepsakes—just his thirty-two pairs of argyle socks and his collection of cotton boxers, his jeans, sneakers, and sweaters and polo shirts. He'd left his suits and his business shirts and the three pairs of leather shoes, which had given off a stench when Caroline burned them all in the backyard later that afternoon, watching the flames flare and glare and crackle and burst.

Now he was back with a 'Hello, Caroline' as if they were meeting for coffee.

'And anyway, I knocked. I knocked a lot. I could hear music and someone moving around inside—is it Simon? It must be Simon—I kept up with the coverage, so I know he's home—but no one answered the door. So I thought I'd wait.'

'Simon doesn't answer the door. He doesn't go out anymore, Geoffrey,' she said in a tone that told him these were important things to know. 'Our son doesn't have a life anymore.'

She bit her tongue and stopped herself from adding: *We don't have a son anymore.*

'I thought … I thought I'd like to see him.'

'You thought? You *thought*?' Her voice began to rise. *Soon only dogs will be able to hear me.* She had to bite down on the giggles that threatened. 'When did you start thinking, Geoffrey, about anyone but yourself?'

'Caroline, I'm sorry—I know I did the wrong thing. It was just so hard—'

'Yes, it fucking was! It was very fucking hard—for me! You just gave up. You just *left*, you shit!'

'Now there's no need for that sort of language . . .'

'You fuck! Fuck you! You leave me to clean up this mess and you're telling me to mind my language? What!? Do you think I'll be a bad influence on Simon?' She let the gate go and turned to fully face him, taking deliberate steps towards him as he backed away.

He paled and she knew he was terrified of her, of this strange new woman who was walking about in her skin. She wondered what he saw in her that made him know she was something different now. She idly wondered if it was the same thing that showed in Simon's face when he—

'I'm sorry, Caroline, this was a bad idea.' She could barely hear him over the sound his keys made as he tried to get them into the car door. She noticed that his vehicle was *old*, no central locking, no blipping noises from electronic entry—no heated seats either, she imagined. A far cry from the Merc he'd driven away in. She wondered what had happened to it, but guessed that if he was trying to visit, he was trying to come back to the comfort of her money. Caroline smiled at him.

He got the door open and put it between them as if it might keep him safe. But he didn't get into the car, he seemed to be about to say something else, and that was his mistake.

Caroline gathered herself, drew upon all the saliva she could muster, and spat in his face. *Pity it's not acid*, she thought, but for his expression it may as well have been. It dripped from the tip of his sharp nose, and slid lazily down his left cheek.

'Don't come back, Geoffrey.'

'WHAT'S THAT?'

Simon dropped the item in question, startled by his mother's sudden appearance. Caroline caught sight of herself in the mirror above his desk. She looked wild, angry, and sick. She stalked into the room. He hunched down and swept the thing up, trying to hide it.

'Nothing,' he grunted. It was the same tone he had used for the last year and she'd thought herself inured to it, but this time she snapped. She swooped on him, shrieking, pushing her face into his until he was almost flat on his mattress as she screamed.

Whatisit, whatisit, whatisit, whatisit?

He threw it on the floor and she stepped back, his movement breaking her tirade. It was a knife. A pocketknife. The one Geoffrey had given him the Christmas before in spite of her objections. The one the police had been unable to find. The one that still had thin brown stains where the blade met the casing.

Time seemed to freeze around them as they stared down at the thing on the blue carpet.

Caroline had steadfastly lied for her son. Yes, he was home that afternoon. No, he had not left his room. They'd had hot chocolate at precisely three o'clock and they had watched cartoons together. No amount of nitpicking or white-anting by the prosecution had shifted or shaken her, and she'd taken a kind of perverse pride in that.

In truth, Caroline didn't really know why she'd lied.

To protect her child, yes, but she didn't understand why she did it when she knew deep down he was guilty. She'd had hope, of course; all mothers have hope beyond hope, a deep abiding belief that a miracle will occur and their child will be proven innocent—because when the guilt is beyond doubt, is known, the world changes irrevocably.

And here it was. Undeniable proof of what he'd done.

Caroline felt something somewhere in her chest give way, cave in, and leave a pile of rubble in its wake. Inside, an already hobbling part of her died.

But it didn't matter. They couldn't charge him again, couldn't retry him. He was out and he'd got away with it.

And he was in her house. He'd come *out* of her. Whatever was in him had come from her.

Slowly she bent down, the cut in her knee reopening, and picked up the knife. Her knuckles turned bone-white around it and she could feel the metal *cutting*. She squeezed her hand tighter, felt satisfied as the blade cut further and blood began to pool in her palm then drip out between her fingers. In the cup of her hand, the new blood liquefied the old, mixed with it.

Caroline lifted her fist and shook it at Simon. Red spattered across his shirt, face, and the blue duvet. Behind his eyes she saw something stir, something that wasn't afraid of her. Not yet.

She moved towards him and the thing inside him began to shift, to squirm. Ah! At last.

Then the window shattered, showering them both with glass, and the spell was broken. Time stumbled forward again. She became aware of the clock in the upstairs hallway, ticking and tocking, reliable as ever. On the bed lay half a brick. Tied to it with a piece of twine was a familiar crumpled square of off-white.

Simon didn't even twitch, still paralysed. Still frozen. Only his eyes swept around, as if looking for escape. Caroline collected the brick, and untied the twine. Resignedly, she pulled the photo away from the rough surface of the concrete carrier pigeon and put it into the pocket of her Barbour. She felt the blood from her hand oozing across the surface, smoothly melting away the emulsion. Caroline straightened, cleared her throat.

'Lunch in ten minutes. If you want food you'll come downstairs like a human being. No more skulking up here. I'm not a zookeeper to keep bringing meals to your door.'

She turned to leave.

'It wasn't anyone important!'

His voice, his words, made her nauseous. She felt hot waves of sick rising, lapping at the back of her throat. She swallowed it down. He wouldn't see—couldn't see—any weakness. Caroline kept moving, towards the door, was almost into the hallway.

'Just a filthy little Rom. Filthy Traveller. Who'd miss him? Mum? Who'd miss him?'

SHE LOCKED the door of her bedroom that night, thought about pushing a set of drawers in front of it, then decided she was being silly. The rage-invigorated woman who had so scared her husband and son seemed to have disappeared. She couldn't, she supposed, burn that brightly for too long. She went to sleep quickly, though, as if all her energy had evaporated. She didn't even take a tablet.

Something woke her in the dark watches.

At first she thought it was Simon and cried out, then remembered he couldn't get in. Anyway, what woke her was a weeping, a whimpering that Simon had never made, not even when he was small.

Her heart clenched when she saw the figure standing solidly black silhouetted on the pale curtains, back-lit by the streetlights.

But she realised the shape, the shadow, was too small.

Caroline sat up slowly and squinted hard into the dimness. Slowly details made themselves known: a patched red sweater, coals cuttle curls, the dirty marks on his face cut by lines of clean where tears had fallen. She didn't turn on the bedside lamp for fear he would disappear. She didn't speak for the same reason.

She offered her hand and held her breath.

He settled beside her under the sheets, beneath the blankets, snuggling into the curve of her as if he belonged there. His skin was so cold she shivered. But she welcomed the sensation—any sensation, any feeling at all that was not despair or contempt or fear or hatred or grief.

The thin little back pressed against her stomach. The little knuckles of the spine stood out and she ran her fingers down them, almost expecting the sound of a xylophone. And he stopped crying. She brushed a hand across his face, felt the still-wet tears and put her fingers to her tongue. They burned, salt and ice, stung her mouth like lemon juice poured into a wound, but she didn't care.

'Mum?' Simon was scratching at the door. 'Mum, are you okay?' He paused. 'It's just I thought I heard you yell . . .'

The child beside her stilled like a small animal trying to escape notice, and then she smelled ammonia. She gathered her breath, kept her voice steady, and said, 'Yes, I'm fine. A dream is all. Go back to bed.'

She listened as his heavy footsteps receded and his bedroom door closed. She could feel the little boy relaxing.

'It's all right,' she whispered. 'It's all right.'

Ignoring the wet stink, the warm damp that was rapidly turning cold, Caroline wrapped her arms around the child and slept soundly.

'I WANT TO GO OUTSIDE,' Simon mumbled through his food.

He wasn't using a knife—she hadn't put one out—and hacked away great chunks of French toast with the edge of his fork, then shovelled each one loaded with disks of banana into his mouth. Syrup dripped down his chin.

Caroline turned back to the stove and deftly flipped over another piece of bread dipped in egg mix. It sizzled as it hit the pan and the smell of heated butter filled her nostrils. She nodded, as if buying herself a few moments. In truth she felt guilty, guiltier than at any other time in her life. She told herself it was because she'd been a bad mother, because she'd feared him, and because of that fear she'd hated him. But it was worse and she knew it.

She hadn't simply hated him. She'd forgotten him. For the briefest of hours she had forgotten him altogether and she had loved another child. Another child who was everything Simon no longer was: vulnerable, innocent. A child who'd filled her need for such a short time. But had done so nevertheless, and in doing so had widened the fractures between Caroline and her son.

So she nodded again and said, 'Where would you like to go?'

'The park? Just out, Mum. Just … out.'

'The park it is, when I finish the dishes. Wrap up, it's cold.'

She could feel, tight by her left leg, the cold weight of the ghost child leaning on her. The small frozen hands gripped her mid-thigh, hampering any movement, but she didn't shift; didn't want to dislodge him, just stayed in place revelling in the sensation of being *essential*.

When Simon finished jamming breakfast into his maw and brought his plate over to the sink, she felt the ghost child dissolve, his presence melt away, leaving only his fear of Simon and a disturbing sense of resentment in Caroline's chest.

It was okay, she thought. It was going to be okay.

The bench was warm beneath her; an unseasonal burst of sun had burned away the chill and the damp and she was toasty in a bubble of light, hidden from the wind by a stand of trees and the toilet block not far behind her. She snuggled down in her coat and closed her eyes for a moment.

The park had been a good idea. Stiff and formal at first, they'd eventually relaxed. Simon had scraped together a tiny, wet ball from remnants of snow (but mostly mud) and thrown it at her. The mark was still visible on her coat; any other time she would have lost her temper, seen it as *mean*, but there was a kind of relief in seeing him behave like a child for the first time in what seemed an age.

It made her remember how it had been when he was small. When loving him wasn't something she thought about, wasn't something she resented, but something she simply *did*; something she did not question. So she laughed and made snow-mud pies of her own and threw them until they were both breathless with laughter and covered with cold, dripping brown.

When she sat to catch her breath, Simon played on the swings. The park started to fill up with other children, but he didn't seem to notice them. More importantly, they didn't appear to notice him. The few parents standing around smoking and watching their own offspring didn't recognise her son either. He took to the slides, then the roundabout, climbed the tree fort, then told her he needed to go to the loo.

She'd smiled and nodded, touched his arm and squeezed to let him know it was going to be okay.

Now she sat, warm and drowsing, as close to happy as she'd been in … she didn't know. They would move, yes. Up north, somewhere with a small school, but close enough to a city with good psychologists; Simon would need help. He would need someone to talk to—as she would, let's face it— someone who could get him to speak about what made him do what he did. Someone who could make him face what he had done, look at it and see it for what it was, and then turn away in disgust—aversion therapy, she thought. He would realise that his choices in future must always turn away from whatever the voice inside him advised. He would recognise his action had been an aberration. He'd acted on a whim, a *curiosity*. It was hideous, terrible, but he had to be allowed to move on. If he didn't, her son would be tied to that awful, awful thing forever.

And so would she.

But they could get past it.

They could work together.

Everything would be okay.

The hand was small and frigid on her face. At first she thought it was Simon, but the hand was too small. Too tender. The touch was sad, tentative, but somehow determined. She moaned *no*, but it didn't help. Caroline didn't want to, but the tiny fingers brushed across her lids, made her blink, let the smallest sliver of daylight in, and she had to come back to the world.

When she opened her eyes, the ghost child was a few feet away. He wasn't looking at her, but staring towards the toilet block. She felt as heavy as she ever had, cemented to the wooden bench, but she heaved herself upwards. Every step was leaden, and she couldn't make herself run. Her legs operated independently of her will and resolutely brought her to the entrance to the male toilets.

The smell of urine assailed her. The floor was tiled and damp. She rounded the corner and peered into the dim-lit rectangular room.

Stalls to the right. A urinal against the far wall. A row of sinks to the left. And in the far corner, her son just visible in the doorway of the furthest stall. Caroline approached quietly, oh so quietly. Behind her she could feel the arctic presence of the ghost child, his little hands holding onto the bottom of her coat. In the moment before Simon sensed her and turned around, she saw into the stall.

An elfin girl this time.

Caroline felt her heart stop, leap, thud like a drum.

The child's face was pinched and pale, but she seemed otherwise unhurt. She was crouched on top of the closed lid of the toilet, curled in on herself like a terrified hedgehog. She looked clean and cared-for in jeans with sequins along the line of the pockets, a pink, puffed jacket, and purple gumboots decorated with flower-shaped raindrops and umbrellas held by black-and-white cows. Not a Traveller's child this time, not a child Simon might think no one would care about. Caroline couldn't help the flare of irritation that after everything that had happened he could be so *stupid*.

The little girl caught sight of Caroline and her mouth opened in a wail of relief and fear.

That was when Simon turned, his eyes widening, pupils dilating, his mouth working like a fish trying to gather breath on land.

'I wasn't! I wasn't doing anything!' He cowered. 'I wasn't going to . . .'

Caroline had thought her son's lies had no more power to hurt her. The moment her hand grasped the collar of his jacket and began to shake him, the girl used the chance to dart out, haring through the tight space between their bodies and the stall door. She let loose a steam train squeal as she passed them by.

Caroline had enough presence of mind to drag him outside and to the car before the shouting started—her own and that of the outraged parents gathering around the little girl who'd made her way to the far side of the park with amazing speed.

In her bathroom, everything was arrayed tidily, in the order she needed.

They had to be ground down, she decided; one simply

couldn't swallow so many any other way. Caroline had taken the boxes from the medicine cabinet, popped the pills out of the blister packs, each one making a satisfying metallic crackle as they broke through the silvery packaging. She'd brought the small mortar and pestle up from the kitchen, the one she kept for dry ingredients, and stood it on the white marble of the vanity unit. She dropped the tablets in, absently counting them as if it mattered, then began the painstaking process of turning them into dust.

In the end, the small mound of white powder wasn't enough. Or perhaps it was, but she didn't really believe it. She wanted to be certain; didn't want to leave anything to chance. Next came the bottles—so many bottles!—the pills larger, harder to crush, but she managed it. She could do it. She could do anything, as long as she concentrated on one task at a time. Behind her, cold radiated, a frigid comfort.

Then the stairs, one at a time, carefully cupping the mortar with both hands. Easy. Down was easiest. One thing at a time.

In the kitchen, she poured milk into a saucepan and put it on the stove, the click of the lighter making her flinch until the gas caught with a blue sigh. From the pantry, the canister, and the sugar bowl. From the cupboard over the sink, a mug, the biggest, his favourite.

The powders, the mixing of white and brown, until no one could tell the difference; the sound of the milk as it heated, simmered, threatened to boil over.

And finally, she stood at the bottom of the stairs, took a breath, kept her voice steady, and called upwards.

'Hot chocolate?'

Winter Children

GRANDMA JO'S eyes light up when she sees me.

'You! You there, girl … boy. Girl?'

Oh, she recognises me, she just doesn't *know* me.

I pin on a smile and approach, tiptoeing through the minefield of rockers, wheelchairs, discarded knee rugs, drooled-upon dolls, magazines opened at half-done crosswords, all manner of old-age home sadnesses scattered across the floor. A sea of faces look up at me expectantly, all of them the same, the rigours of age rendering them alike.

Gypsy, the home's resident dog—in actual fact she belongs to Mrs Buddenbaum, but a lot of days Mrs B forgets she owns a dog, so the shih-tzu shares her love around to anyone who'll give her a pat—barks loudly. She's outside in the yard for her morning ramble, which generally consists of crapping on the most-likely-to-be-walked-on piece of grass and trying desperately to get back inside where there are tummy scratches, old people to feed her pieces of chocolate, cardigan-pocket-softened caramels, occasional meds, and a lot of other things not meant to be consumed by animals. Gypsy, it must be said, is basically a junkie with an accompanying sugar dependency. She also has an unhealthy fondness for me.

I have to time my visits to make sure she's outside or she will not leave me alone, demanding attention and never-ending pats. Six months of pretending I like dogs is almost over. I move past the nursing staff, exchange frozen grins. Once, I worried someone might recognise me, but no. It's been too long.

'Don't know why that animal likes you so much, missy,' Grandma Jo says, sure now that I'm a girl, although she eyes my very short hair in a disapproving manner.

'Guess I'm just special,' I say and lean down to give her a peck on the cheek. 'It's Kirsty, by the way.'

'I know,' she snaps, but I can see the relief in her face that she doesn't have to *remember*. She smells like talcum powder and lily of the valley eau de cologne. They've set her hair today or yesterday and the curls are still tight and white. You know the urge you get to write in wet cement? Well, I get the same kind of urge when I see curls like these—except I want to touch them and feel the springiness. Past experience has shown she gets cranky when I do that, so I don't. 'How are you going, Grandma Jo?'

'Not going anywhere, obviously,' she says waspishly. She puts a hand against her cheek, letting her fingers catch in each furrow, as if wondering where the lines came from. I saw the photo she keeps in her room, of when she got married; she was so beautiful she looked like a work of art. Who'd have thought it would fade away, that beauty? Not her. I think about this every time *I* look in the mirror and remind myself *Nothing's permanent, certainly not life.*

'Well, I thought, maybe we could.'

'What?' she asks. 'What do you mean? You're not making sense and what's with that stupid haircut? Do you want to look like some kind of lesbian?'

She's not actually *my* grandmother, so I don't have to take this kind of shit.

'You old bat. Who do you think you are?' I take a breath, trying be *nice*, patient with an old woman's foibles. 'I'll thank you to shut it or I won't be taking you on any excursions.'

She shrinks, curls up like a spider for a moment, then turns on the biggest of smiles and her hair seems to positively *glow* and fluff before my very eyes. Some animals make themselves bigger to intimidate predators. Grandma Jo makes herself cuter. I sit next to her, giving her a sideways glance. Her face is a picture of expectation.

'What kind of excursion, Kirsty?' she almost trills and I nod approval; *Good girl*.

'Oh, just a drive, I thought. Maybe go into town for coffee and cake, maybe drive to a park and sit on the swings for a while?'

Her smile widens. 'Can we have ice cream?'

'If you behave.'

Her face clouds over. 'But you'll bring me back here.'

I lean in close and say very quietly, 'No, Josephine. Tonight I won't bring you back here.'

And her expression is a sunburst, the brightest thing I've seen in a long dark time. 'Shall I pack a bag?'

I shake my head. 'Nope. We'll get everything you need later. Nothing for you to worry about.'

She settles in her chair, wiggles into the depths of the sheepskin rug, and looks contented as a cat.

I stand and touch her shoulder. 'I'll be back later this afternoon, okay? Can you be waiting outside at five-thirty? Just after you have dinner?'

'Where are you going?' she demands.

'I've got some things to do. So, after your dinner, wait for me on the ring road around the back, okay? And be subtle.'

'I *know* how to sneak out, young lady.'

We nod at each other, satisfied, each thinking ourselves smarter than the other. There's a commotion at the door to the garden—Gypsy is throwing herself at the thick glass and one of the attendants is making her way over to let the thing in. Mrs Buddenbaum is glaring at the dog as if she doesn't recognise it at all.

Exit, Kirsty, stage right.

GRANDMA JO DOESN'T BELIEVE in incognito.

She's standing beside the bay where the ambulance parks, wearing Greta Garbo sunglasses that cover half of her face, a floppy straw hat, a scarf long enough to give Isadora Duncan nightmares, and some kind of drapey lounging outfit which may, in fact, be pink chiffon pyjamas. Her handbag, in conjunction with gravity, is working to overbalance her. I pull up and lean over to open the door before they win.

She gets into the car in a manner that can be described as either stately or god-awful slow, depending on your upbringing.

I'm calm, just a granddaughter collecting her nanna for a bit of a drive. Doesn't matter if anyone sees me; after this trip I'll be gone, no more than the dust of a memory. Grandma Jo has no family, no one to go looking for her. The home will put in the required paperwork, but they've got enough living ghosts to take care of, haven't they?

'Ice cream,' she says first off.

I raise my eyebrows and she remembers to add, 'Please?'

She's like an excited pup, head turning this way and that, trying to drink in all the sights before the sun goes down and her eyes can't quite function as they need to, as they used to. Grandma Jo is happy, all white teeth, not denturey at all. The sun drops below the horizon and the last burst of golden-orange fire makes her eyes light up red and huge.

Then the afternoon flame is gone and she's ordinary again, a little old lady with eccentric taste in escape attire.

I remember these streets. Nothing seems to have changed; when I turn left, I don't find a new cul de sac, or street pacifiers; no new housing developments.

When I first came back, I found the outskirts of town existing in the same strange limbo world, part rural, part suburban: farmhouses with wide porches at the front and designer barns out back, tidy white fences bordering big lots; each property not too close and not too far away from the next one over. When I'd put the key into the door of my parents' empty house, it still turned in the lock. They travel a lot nowadays—I get postcards, picking them up from a variety of PO boxes around the country—but they can't seem to get rid of the place. The furniture was all where it had been, the smell was different though, dead air and dust. A lot of the houses around it were empty, too, victims of the economic downturn—when I'd walked around in the dusk I could see how dilapidated some had become. That and the distance between farmhouses meant I didn't have to worry too much about being spotted.

'So,' I say, trying not to act as though I'd forgotten she was there, 'the park and ice cream? Dessert first, hey?'

'Delightful. All those years of having to eat my mains first and now I can please myself for a change. When I was a child, it was always no pudding if you don't eat your vegetables … or was it?' Her voice quavers with uncertainty. 'Was there food? Enough food?'

I wonder what else she might remember, away from the atmosphere of the home, away from the regimen of pills, the cocktail of things to calm you down, pick you up, make you sleep, wake you up, keep your bowels regular, lower your blood pressure, thin your blood.

But her smile is sweet and has no depths, nothing hidden, nothing remembered.

All kinds of things can forget what they were; what they are.

I pull up near the cafe, the overpriced one with the bored teenager serving a limited night menu for the next couple of hours. *Brit'nee*, her badge insists, as she turns her listless attention from the young couple ahead of us (he overweight and spotty and she really quite lush) and takes our order, scrupulously not making eye contact.

Grandma Jo is distracted by the ice cream cone *Brit'nee* hands over—bubblegum flavour—and gives it a tentative lick. Her mouth twists askew and *this doesn't taste quite right* is written all over her face. She frowns at the treat then is diverted by something else—the girl is flipping raw, compacted, circular meat onto the grill.

Red seeps up and out, turns brown on the hot metal plate. She uses an ancient wooden-handled meat cleaver to hack at an onion, and thin translucent slices of white join the sizzling circles, sending out mouth-watering fumes. Grandma Jo's eyes light up.

'Burger!' she says.

Brit'nee gives me a flat look and I nod. 'You want fries with that?'

'I want the lot!'

'Make it two,' I tell Brit'nee and hand over more money. My wallet is feeling thin, a little anorexic. About time for an injection, I'd say. Grandma Jo's earrings would go for a pretty penny and her pearl necklace, if I'm not mistaken.

We take up metal seats that are cold without the sun. The table between us is rickety, designed that way, I'm sure, by someone with a grudge against public eateries. I stuff a handful of paper napkins under one leg—which stops the wobbling from east to west but causes more wobbling north to south. I give up.

The dusk-dimmed lawn rolls gently down a slope in front of us, to a play area dotted with swings and seesaws, plastic and metal spring animals, contraptions that go round and round really fast and make you want to vomit. And there are the cages—aviaries; habitats for koala, possum and wallaby; petting zoos for goats, sheep and calves—and koi ponds, shallow and murky with the occasional bright orange flash among the water plants, here and gone so quickly you doubt you saw it. A gentle breeze lifts the old lady's curls and then moves on to the leaves and branches of the trees.

'This is nice,' Grandma Jo says. 'Oh, so nice. I haven't been out in a very long time.'

'Glad you like it,' I reply, thinking that everyone deserves a last day out.

'You're not my granddaughter,' she confides as if she's just letting me in on a secret.

I nod. 'I know. Never said I was.'

'Fibber. You told the nurses at the home you were.'

'I may have been careless with the truth,' I agree.

'I don't mind. It's just so nice to be out.'

I don't say anything because Brit'nee brings over our burgers and bangs the plates down hard on the tabletop so the fries do a little dance as if they're making a break for freedom. Grandma Jo makes a grab for her burger, bites down through the inflated bun, tearing through tomato, onion, lettuce, an egg and into the meat patty, which is burnt on the outside and pink on the inside. Crimson-brown juice spurts —or maybe that's beetroot?—and the white teeth turn an arresting shade of pink.

My appetite deserts me faster than a deadbeat dad on child-support day. I eat half a chip, push the plate away. The old lady helps herself to my food when hers is gone, without so much as a by-your-leave. I look away, down towards the swings, where two small kids are still playing, seemingly unattended by any adults. I think of my sister on the swing that hung from the tree marking the boundary between two properties. It makes me nervous and angry, that people are so careless with their kids, so ignorant of what lives in the dark. Wilfully ignorant.

'Aleksandr loved burgers,' she says, pushing her dead husband's name out around the last mouthful. Little shreds of lettuce fly across the table. 'He was a meat man.'

'I bet. Where did you meet?'

'He was so handsome. He was a Russian soldier and I was a Red Cross nurse.' She frowns. 'Wasn't I?'

'Your story.'

'I remember cold. I remember snow.' The trace of an accent creeps in and I don't suppose I expected that. I've looked for her for so long, but I can't remember if she had one before.

'Grandma Jo, where were you born?'

'Me? Why here, of course. But I travelled. Yes, I went so many places.' The accent is stronger. 'Didn't I?'

I watch her talk almost to herself, picking through lies and memories and trying to knit them together. 'I had a family, so many brothers and sisters, all of us fighting for food, fighting so hard . . .'

Then it fades. I can see it in her face, remembrances dissolving one by one like candles blown out at bedtime. Around us, the night is suddenly heavy and empty and she's a sweet old lady with pale blue eyes and a gentle lost sort of smile.

'I need to powder my nose,' she announces. The sign for the toilets indicates they are attached to the cafe, the entrance just along the side wall and I point. She makes her way with a tottering elegance, clutching her handbag, towards the bathrooms. The door closes behind her with a whisper.

I lean forward, rubbing my eyes until I see stars against the black of my lids. *Am I right? Is this a mistake? Have I been tracking so long that I no longer see the signs? Have I gone blind to what's in front of me? Do I now imagine danger in every shadow, see a monster in every pensioner I meet? All those times I've never doubted. How many have there been before this one? The one that started everything?*

The night is so quiet, just the distant rumble of cars and the last creaks of the now-deserted swing set. I feel as if my sister sits at my shoulder, but when I open my eyes there's nothing, no one.

I look about—the young couple moved off long ago and *Brit'nee* is applying a premature end-of-night enthusiasm to cleaning the grill.

Making my way to the toilets, I push the door open. Grandma Jo is washing her hands, handbag pooled on the slightly grubby floor at her feet. The light from the naked bulbs on the ceiling makes her hair shine silvery-purple. She looks up and sees me in the mirror.

I stand behind her and smile, finding the hanging ends of her long silky scarf and entwining them in my fingers. 'What a lovely scarf, Grandma Jo.'

She smiles back until she feels the silk tightening.

But she doesn't raise her hands, doesn't struggle. Doesn't do anything while her eyes start to bulge, tongue protrudes, lips go a little bluer in the bathroom lights. She's not heavy as I let her slowly slip to the ground. Grandma Jo makes a very small pile in the corner of the stall. I close the door, lock it, then stand on the toilet lid and heave myself over the top.

The handbag is on the tiles, soaked in a combination of water and urine. I open it and dig carefully around inside. Three rolls of peppermints, a can of mace, a variety of keys, a coin purse, a pair of support hose all wrapped up, and then the book. A diary, with a battered cover.

But it doesn't look the way my memory says it should. It's blue, not brown. There's no gold on the edges of the paper. No leather ties to hold the thing together. Maybe I misremember. It's been a long time.

I flip the book open.

Notes in a blue pen, sometimes a red pen. The handwriting grows worse, more spidery as the dates progress, the notes less comprehensible. And no photos. Not a one.

Nothing that's supposed to be there.

A weight that might be Grandma Jo presses on my chest, surprisingly heavy for a little old lady.

Back at the home: it must be there, in a drawer, under neatly folded clothes or in the top of a wardrobe. It has to be there.

IN THE EAST wing there are rooms that are dark because their inhabitants are asleep, others because they're simply empty. In fact, the east wing is the least populated part of the home—only for the moment, a brief ebb tide in the population. Grandma Jo's door is closed, but not locked. No one, it seems, has realised she's missing yet. There are no police cars out the front of the building, no rushing panicking staff, no administrator racing around like a bureaucratic chicken trying to cover up the careless loss of an *inmate*.

I close the door behind me and flick the switch. The space is bathed in yellow light. There's a thin bed with a pastel-pink doona and a crocheted rug at the foot, a brown rocker-recliner, a bank of photos cover one wall—all Grandma Jo and Aleksandr—a leadlight cabinet filled with crystal, commemorative spoons, and porcelain dolls. A tall stack of drawers stands next to the long glass window. I pull open the top one and start going through the neat shirts and light cardigans. In between the folds of fabric are necklaces, rings, and bracelets and earrings, all of which would pay my way for long months. But I don't stop to pocket them, I keep digging, one drawer after the next.

In the last one there's still nothing. I turn towards the cupboard and the weight on my chest is getting heavier, growing like a stain on a carpet.

'"I had a family, so many brothers and sisters, all of us fighting for food, fighting so hard, so hungry and so cold. We walked the white and so few of us came out. I was strong . . ." Did she say that?'

I didn't even hear the door. A woman's voice, and old; she's only a silhouette against the open doorway.

I nod. 'Some of it.'

'I taught her. So many times, I made her say it over and over and she cried, but I promised her, I promised if she did it someone would rescue her. Someone would take her away.' Laughter lifts the voice and Mrs Buddenbaum steps into the dim room. 'You took her away, didn't you, Kirsty?'

I feel a chill limbo its way down my spine.

'I find it useful to have some camouflage.' She sniggers. 'I remember frozen meat and red on white . . .' she says and I feel myself fall out of time. I remember my sister there one day, gone the next. I remember red on the white of the snow, and limbs frozen in place.

She goes on, 'Your sister was *sweet*.' She steps back out and I follow her, slowly, along the quiet corridor.

In her room, she takes up residence in a rocking chair. 'How did you find me?'

'Cold trails. Reports of missing children. Nothing that got me here very fast.'

'Oh, but you were only—what, eight when we met? You couldn't have done much for years after that.'

'I watched a lot of news. A lot of crime alert shows. I kept scrapbooks.'

'Like this?' The tiny little octagonal coffee table beside her has a drawer in the front. She reaches in and pulls out a heavy leather-bound book.

This is exactly as I remember.

She opens the cover and leafs through thoughtfully, each page covered with children's photographs, some family snapshots stolen from grieving homes, some neatly clipped from newspapers. It looks like a diary, but I know it for what it was: a menu.

'Ah, yes.' She gently peels out a photo, smaller than it should be, one half torn away, and holds it up. My sister, aged nine, smiles back at me. Her arms lead to the ragged edge of the paper, cut off at the forearm. In the space that's gone is where I once was.

'It was so good of you to give me this. I do like to have my memories all in the one place.'

She'd said, back in the old days when her name was, however briefly, Lily Powers—Aunty Lil to the neighbourhood —that she wanted photos of her special friends. I gave it to her three days before my sister disappeared. If I let my eyes lose focus a little, let things blur the wrinkles on her face, let this little deception strip away the last twenty years, I can see it. I can see the nice lady who rented the house next door at the end of summer, baked cookies for us, and made real lemonade, then one day took my sister's life and disappeared just as quickly in the night before anyone knew.

When my sister was seen again, it was in small pieces, in patches of red on white.

I swallow. All these memories, coming back here—it's

made me stupid. I'm unarmed, all my lovely sharp things left in the boot of the car because I was sure I'd taken out the monster.

'How many?' We ask the question at the same time.

'Age before beauty,' I say and she grins.

'That's the spirit! Ever wonder why I took her and not you? Why I took little Sally?' She waves the photo, makes it look as though it's walking in the air. 'Because she was sweet and you were not. Even then, you were a sour little troll.'

'Takes one to know one,' I tell her, but my heart twists. I *had* wondered for so long and with so much guilt and with that tiny, stupid, insane little echo of *why not me?* 'How many?'

'Hundreds. Thousands? So many years, so many meals.' She shrugs, gestures at the diary. 'And you? '

'A lot,' I say. A lot of strange blood between then and now. 'A lot of your kind out there, more than people might think.'

'And how many mistakes? How many Grandma Joes?'

I ignore that. 'Why come back here? Didn't you worry someone might recognise you?'

'Did you? But I recognised you,' she singsongs as if she's caught me out. 'That bitter little mouth, those dark angry eyes. Never fear, no one else would know you, no one else watches like me.'

My hands are shaking.

'I have so enjoyed our chat. Nothing lasts forever, though, does it?' She stands and offers me the photo. 'I suppose I knew my run would come to an end someday.'

Disarmed, I step across the room and reach for the photo. My fingers touch the torn edge and Mrs B grabs my wrist.I find myself on my back, the photo fluttering away on the air. My head rests against Mrs B's surprisingly hard thigh and her stringy arm is wrapped around my throat. A cold hard sharpness presses against the flesh. 'But not today.'

The blade bites and my blood trickles warmly.

'Pity you're too old for me now, I do so hate waste.'

More pressure for a second and then it's gone and a smelly, silky mass bounds up my body and sinks its teeth into Mrs B's wrist. The dog hangs on for dear life until the Swiss Army knife goes flying and the old lady manages to dislodge the animal. Gypsy hits the wall with the same noise as a squeaky toy and lies still.

I roll over, gasping for breath.

Outside there are sounds of stirring. I struggle to my feet. The room is empty. On the floor lies the photo of my sister and, not far from it, the pocketknife, its blade slick and dark. I pocket them both and fly out the door.

Blood tracks along the white corridor, through the day room and out the patio doors. The gate meant to keep the inhabitants in is hanging off its hinges. How fast is she? How strong?

Out the gate and left, past my car. Ahead of me I can see a white blur in the darkness moving into the stretch of nature reserve on the other side of the road. I follow.

Deep in the trees, with beams of moonlight streaking through the branches, I can't make out much, but I can hear her, crashing ahead of me. Then, quiet. I keep moving. Branches reach out and scratch at my face. Somewhere close by an animal has died and is busy rotting.

A snapping sound, then heavy breathing and the sensation of being hit from the side, knocking the air from my lungs. I fall, my nose and mouth filling with a combination of dirt and grass. I roll over as quickly as I can, spitting and coughing, but she's on my chest in a flash.

The old bitch leans in, eyes bulging and lined with darkest red, face smoothed of all wrinkles, and mouth opened wide as wide can be, lined with two rows of teeth, shiny-sharp.

I wonder if this was the last thing my sister saw, all those years ago, when the snow came and something walked through the white and turned her into a red smear on the pristine ground. Something that transformed them into winter children and left ragged remnants behind to mark their passing.

Long-fingered hands press at my throat, tightening, the nails sawing into my flesh. Little explosions are happening at the edges of my vision and I can feel the blood flowing from the gashes in my throat. In my pocket is the weight of the knife, painfully imprinting its shape into my skin, impossible to get to with Mrs B on top of me.

My left hand is trying to pry her fingers away from my throat; the right is scratching around in the dirt, desperately seeking, finding a large stick, a small branch. Sharp enough, sturdy enough, I hope—I pull it back, trying to get as much force behind it as I can and then jam it into her side. For a few seconds the flesh resists, then the pointy end pushes in, makes a sound and *she* makes a sound. I twist the stick, getting it further and further in. I angle it upwards and her grip loosens. I imagine I hear a *pop* somewhere in her chest and her mouth opens to emit a sigh, laden with nothing so much as disappointment.

Mrs B slumps on top of me.

I slide her to the side and claw my way upwards, standing, swaying, staring down at her vacant eyes, at the two tows of teeth still gleaming in the moonlight. I look down at my boots with their steel caps.

At first I kick and feel the side of the head cave in. I switch to stomping and watch her face dissolve into a mess of crushed flesh and fractured bones. The blood looks black in the moonlight.

I limp back to my car, open the door, and sit down—half-in, half-out, gingerly breathing as my ribs protest. The trickle of blood around my throat is already slowing, going from slick to sticky. I lean my head back, close my eyes.

Time to get out of town. Time to leave. No time to go back to my parents' and pick up the few pieces of clothing I left. No one will look there. My parents won't be home any year soon.

In the darkness, something licks my shin and I just about piss my pants. I kick out and connect with a furry softness, but all I hear is an apologetic whimper. Gypsy limps into the splash of light thrown from the car's interior and licks at me again. It's her mistress's blood, I guess.

I have no choice but to pick her up.

She curls on the passenger seat and goes to sleep, the scent of slightly damp dog filling the vehicle. I'll get her to a vet as soon as I can; between me and Mrs B, she'll need some attention.

I turn the key in the ignition and listen for a moment to the rumble of the engine. It's the sort of sound to keep monsters at bay. I peel off into the night, unsure if I feel lighter or lost.

There are always places to get lost.

Pale Tree House

'ANDERSON, you are to collect a consignment for Pale Tree House. Mr Holloway has requirements once again.'

Mr Plum handed me a thin envelope; inside was the address of an orphanage in ——shire, and more than sufficient funds to cover my travel costs. I would pocket the remainder, he understood. The delivery location, I knew full well after thirteen years. I set off. With a steady pace I could make the last train out of Victoria.

A mystery to some, how I came by a position in such a fine and upstanding firm of solicitors. My university record was patchy at best; no recorded fails due more to my knowledge of matters the masters did not wish spoken aloud rather than any great scholarly diligence of my own. I had gotten through by dishonesty, rat cunning, and the smallest possible amount of study.

Mr Plum of ——son & Partners, an old friend of my despairing father, saw something useful in me. My tasks were those no one else would undertake: parcels of uncertain provenance with questionable contents, negotiations with shadowy men, the supply of unusual services to clients of particular needs and spectacular means. The agency's reputation was twofold: the sunlit path and that of moonlight. I, Anderson James, represented the former.

Someone had to do it.

'The moneys have already been deposited in our trust account, an impressive amount even for *this*,' Mr Plum had said with a satisfied air.

I HAD a first-class carriage to myself and closed my eyes as soon as we pulled out. I generally sleep well no matter where I am, but there was a lingering cold despite the summer night and my tweed frock coat was unequal to the chill. I did but doze fitfully.

It was well past midnight by the time I reached village of Otterburn in ——shire, but I walked the short distance from my stop, the full moon clearly lit the road before me. When I rounded the corner and espied my goal, I was taken aback. A large structure: two floors and an attic high, tall windows running its length. It looked almost worse than I could have believed—derelict. Although orphanages, like workhouses, are not places of luxury, this one seemed not merely asleep but deserted. Except for the small white figure crouched on the front stoop. As I approached she rose.

This child's face was *familiar*—but I could not recall her precisely, and I remembered them all, you see. Perhaps eight years old, white skin, pale eyes in darkened sockets, thin-limbed, a wheat-coloured dress, scuffed shoes. She was clean and neat, though, with blue ribbons wound through her plaits.

'They told me to wait out here,' she said, unafraid.

'Good girl. It seems rather late, though.'

'I do what Mrs Bickersby tells me.'

A happy tendency, and Mrs Bickersby's actions quite

credible—good women did not generally run such establishments as these.

'Then let us not delay.' I picked up the bag at her feet, finding it light, and offered my hand. I peered closely, trying to place her, but no child was ever delivered twice.

'What if I don't like it?' she asked. '*There?*'

I said what I always say: 'Then write me at my firm. I am Mr James and I will come for you, I promise. Be so kind as to wait.'

She nodded, seemingly mollified, almost as if it was what she expected.

We had several hours pause at the station and she slept, curled on a wooden bench. When the train arrived, I carried her on board, settling her on the plush seat and allowing her to slumber still. I did not imagine she had ever slept so comfortably. *One last treat*, I thought as we travelled north.

Mr Holloway was a client with specific annual needs. I neither understood nor shared his tastes, but appreciated that he paid well, and kept a buggy and beast at the local stables for visits such as mine. A high wall surrounded Pale Tree House's large park; a bleached oak sat in front of the abode.

My knock echoed inside, yet there was no answer. I found the door unlocked, so we stepped in. The moment the door closed behind us I felt a great sense of unease—conscience? —such as has never before troubled me.

The child let go of my hand and moved away, into a shadowed corner of the entry hall. She began to glow bluish-white, and her face became more sharply defined.

And I realised that those features belonged not to one child, but to all those I had ever delivered here. My memory had not failed me, but rather been tricked by juxtaposition.

'We will come for you, Mr James, we promise. Be so kind as to wait,' said the child, the children, as they split apart and became their separate selves, twelve pairs of eyes steady upon me. They each disappeared, silent as the grave, leaving me to wait and sweat and wonder when they will return.

I have tried the doors and windows and all are sealed tight by some unbreakable will. I threw a chair at a window, only to have it rebound and strike hard enough to leave a bruise. I can find no trace of Mr Holloway; I can but imagine his fate caught him some time since.

I would not be surprised if the moneys over which Mr Plum gloated have disappeared, tricksy as fairy gold. I leave this letter in case anyone should come looking for me, which I consider unlikely. My father will be relieved at my disappearance and Mr Plum will soon find another such as me.

There it is: the creak of the study door. Such drama, these little ghosts, such spite. I will question them, as they take revenge. I suspect they will not answer, not for a century or two, just to teach me. To teach me to be so kind as to *wait*.

The Red Forest

THE CHURCH behind the house is deserted, neglected, and has been for some time. It's made of wood that is bowed and splintered, silvered by the elements. Truth be told, thinks Dina, the one a little way down the road near Yolkov's farm isn't in much better repair nowadays, even though it's newer. Mind you, no one much uses that one anymore either, only occasional tramps, scouting parties and the like.

It's simpler than the great ones across the border, with their bright colours and cupola-topped towers. This one is an immigrants' church, made without much money, but much devotion, three levels and a tall spire, the onion dome unadorned. Uncle Abram said it used to be covered in gold, once, when it was first raised, but Uncle Abram also used to keep pigeons in there before he died; after he died too. Dina sometimes still sees him or what's left of him, tending to the birds that have stayed, the ones that are getting old, have lost their sense of direction, or simply can't be bothered going anywhere else. He's a kind of silver-grey now, Uncle Abram, as he flits around the disused machinery and the rusting truck bodies that gradually replaced the pews; he's less substantial than he was in life, which is some achievement since he was as thin as a twig then. Aunt Varvara used to say, when she still had the wherewithal to say anything, that he'd end up in the next town over if a strong wind blew through.

Of course she's gone too, Aunt Varvara, carried off by the sickness that swept through the Valley, one of the first to go despite the deal she'd struck, thinking to ward if off. They'd found no hope in the light, been offered no deliverance despite all their prayers, all that wasted time spent on their knees in the church, all the tiny bloody sacrifices that brought them nothing.

In the end salvation of a sort had come from the very darkness itself.

DINA CAN HEAR the distant growl of tanks as she washes her lonely cup and bowl; the coffee and porridge were unsatisfying, even tinged red as they were with the last of her supplies. The soldiers are coming because they're always coming, crossing borders that shift from one day to the next, taking and losing countries that have their names changed without warning. Dina's not sure what her nation's called anymore. The soldiers are coming, but they're still far off. Dina can tell by the sound, the echoes and rumbles, the way the air trembles only a little. They'll be searching, no doubt, for the others. She has time.

She climbs the stairs to the attic room she used to share with her cousins. It's been all hers for a while now. The dress is laid out on the bed that once accommodated four girls of various heights and girths. Irina and Klara were no trouble, but Zoya took up a lot of space, farted a lot too. Were she to be truthful, Dina would say she wasn't entirely unhappy to see the back of Zoya when her time came, to see her buried in her own white dress with the tiny purple flowers she'd insisted on embroidering along the hem. She had a fine hand, Zoya, for such things. The other girls had begged her help and she'd agreed in return for their share of dessert—when there were still such luxuries to go around—for six months. Irina and Klara had readily agreed; they were used to such bargains with their sister.

As her daughters disappeared one by one, Aunt Varvara drew closer to Dina; she'd always been fond of her niece, her dead brother's orphaned child. When it came time for Dina's white dress, Aunt Varvara had done most of the sewing, though tradition decreed a girl should make her own wedding gown. She'd done it in spite of Dina's illness, in spite of all the predictions that the girl would not live past her sixteenth birthday, that no man would have such a sickling to wife. She wouldn't be able to provide children —*sons*—wouldn't be able to keep a house. Any man who married Dina would find himself tending her as if she were a sick child, be unmanned by *nursing*.

No husband would choose that.

Dina didn't care about the dress, indeed had no skills for such a thing even if she desired it. But Varvara would not have a bar of her protests, nor anyone's naysaying. She constructed the gown at night, sat Dina beside her, made her sew the seams, the parts inside where no one would look, so that the girl's hands at least touched the frock, made some contribution to its birth. But all the fancy work, all the complicated frilling and shirring, embroidery and fitting—all of that was Varvara's genius. Once upon a time, there would have been so many bright colours, so much embroidery in so many hues, an outfit of festive wedding wealth with a headdress to bend a bride's neck, but Western bridal magazines—stolen, traded, fought over—had brought new ideas, encouraged that custom be put aside. The gown is entirely white, even the hand-stitched flowers, picked out in expensive silk thread that Dina's mother had set by so many years ago, and which Varvara had rescued from the burning house along with Dina—after ascertaining her brother and sister-in-law were beyond help—and kept secure for her niece.

Dina stares at it affectionately, remembering the nights by the fire with her aunt—remembering, with a fondness she did not feel at the time, each pinprick, each hand slap for her carelessness. She recalls instead that her aunt believed she, Dina, would live. Would survive and thrive and need just such a dress. She reaches out, but her fingers don't make contact with the fabric, not yet.

Instead, she looks to the window with its diamond-shaped panes, again towards the old church; its unhealthy slant has become worse if she's not very badly mistaken. It was a beautiful thing, even with glass gone from the frames, and the endless trailing lace of bird shit streaking from the onion dome down the spire and the walls. The wooden tiles look like dragon scales or aggressive nettle leaves; either way, they bristle, defensive about their parlous state. But it is old, past its time, and not everything gets to live on, become something new.

She can see the luminous flicker that is Uncle Abram, passing back and forth in front of the empty casements, somehow with birdseed held in his ephemeral hands. No point in saying goodbye; he won't hear her, or see her ... or he'll pretend he doesn't, much as it was when he breathed. Dina misses Aunt Varvara, though, and wonders why of the two she wasn't the one to come back. Even if only to nag Dina about brushing her hair and making sure her shirt was properly pressed and tucked into her skirt.

Beside the building is the graveyard, so small it seems hard to believe how many bodies it swallowed. Dina had nursed Abram and Varvara, her cousins, and more than a dozen of their nearest neighbours. At first she'd had help but eventually there was no one else left. People had come to the Kozlov farm in search of aid—at one point there'd been ten invalids on makeshift beds in the living room and the kitchen —but they grew sicker still. They'd found not a cure, just a kind hand to tend them as they died. *Surely not a thing to be sniffed at*, thought Dina.

As with the nursing, there'd been aid to start with when the cycle turned to burying, but as folk sickened they lost both the will and the ability to swing a shovel, and she was left alone to do the interments. The last couple, Dina had to admit, weren't too deep under the sparse new grass. She was healthier, stronger by then, and her hands had toughened, the palms no longer blistering from the spade's handle; however, she just didn't have the energy to go down the six feet Father Gribov had insisted on before he got too ill to do anything but shit in his sheets. He'd been the last one she'd planted—had *encouraged* him on his way with a pillow over the face when he was too weak to protest, too weak to do anything but tell her that she was a bad person, evil, damned; that her aunt had been the same. He wasn't a pleasant man. There was nothing kindly or generous or forgiving about him. She used to think he wasn't a good churchman, dominating the Valley folk from the tiny church down the road, the one where the walls didn't bow, the ceiling didn't house pigeons, where the windows were still intact, but nowadays Dina suspected he was *precisely* that: a good churchman. Just not a good human being. Maybe that was why his religion failed him, failed all of them.

Or perhaps his flock had simply been trained to believe kindness wasn't to be expected of God. Perhaps that was why, when Varvara brought them her solution, they took the hand that was offered, no matter that it was blackened and bore nails that might be mistaken for talons. Perhaps, when you can see death coming, you'll do anything to avoid it and not be too picky about the details.

Dina's eyes drift to the other grave, the one that's just outside the graveyard's low iron fence. This one was buried well; Dina had not taken part in this inhumation. She had still been recovering, lying in the bed in the attic, though she propped herself up that night, watched through the window as they interred the old woman by torchlight. As they dug deep, deep down to make sure she stayed where she was put.

DINA'S FINGERS ARE THIN, the nails sharper than they used to be, her skin rougher. As she undoes her blouse, the cicatrix on her chest is exposed. One button at a time, seemingly such a small action to show such a dreadful trauma. Red, thick, raised, almost new enough that she can see the thin line where the cut was made. So fine a slice to have produced such a large scar! She'd been given some of Aunt Varvara's poppy milk to make her sleep that night, but sometimes she's sure she remembers the sensation of that incision, of the creaking farm implements repurposed to spread her ribs wider and wider—some days they still ache— the feeling of Aunt's small fingers, tiny palm, closing around her heart . . .

The old woman had come to them, wandered out of the forest that backed onto the Kozlov's farm. She'd knocked at the door, begged food, drink, eyed Dina, who'd risen from bed only to recline on the threadbare sofa by the fire, pale and wasting as her heart unhurriedly betrayed her. The old baba ate slowly, mostly gumming the fresh bread Aunt Varvara gave her, dipping it into the warm milk as if it wasn't soft enough; as if it wasn't the only thing they had to offer. Food was scarce by then, everywhere, yet they gave of what they had. Dina could see that the old woman's distaste annoyed her aunt, but Varvara was smart enough not to make complaint. No good ever came of upsetting forest wives, which was why they'd welcomed her into their home even as tales of the sickness coming closer swept in on the breath of travellers and traders. Even though their friends and family had already begun to decrease in number.

The baba's skin was a mass of crevices, as if she'd been the site of some dreadful geological event. Her hair was black but wiry and bushy beneath the red scarf, and her eyes were also black but sometimes in the light of the fire Dina thought there might be an undercurrent of yellow, like piss or spite. She wore so many skirts and shawls it was impossible to know what shape she was beneath them all—a riot of colours once, now faded and muted by time and dirt.

When Aunt Varvara went outside to hang the washing, the old woman sidled over to Dina, sat at her feet, felt the toes beneath the blanket to see how cold they were.

'How long do you have, girl?' she croaked.

Dina shrugged. 'I don't know.'

'How long have you been dying?'

'Forever.'

The old woman grunted. Nodded. She put her hand against the girl's chest and Dina was too weak to shake her off, too tired to shout for Varvara's help. But the crabbed digits with their swollen knuckles and sharp nails went no further, did nothing but lay against the place where Dina's heart gave its lethargic *lub-dubs*. Then the old woman nodded again, grunted again, and took her fingers away.

'My heart,' she crackled. 'My heart is strong. So strong. It's my body that's giving up. Now you, the body is *sound*, but that treacherous heart is going to kill you.'

Dina hadn't answered, just stared into the flames of the hearth.

When Aunt Varvara returned, the old woman rose and

went to her. Spoke low, coaxed her to a corner of the kitchen where Dina could not hear them. Her aunt's voice never rose in either anger or fear or hope, but when Varvara came to her a few hours later, having done the rounds of the Valley with the old woman in tow, she was pale and exhausted-looking, lines drawn on her face that had never been there before.

And then she told Dina what the old woman, the baba —*the* Baba—had proposed. What the folk of the Valley had agreed.

DINA TOUCHES THE SCAR; the raised red flesh still feels hot, but perhaps that's because she was so used to bad circulation all her life, to the cold. The new heart pushes blood around her body as the old never did. Varvara had taken the old woman's offer, thinking to save her niece and all those who starved and sickened around them. That the Baba's gift might stop their crops from failing, their children from dying, the soldiers from marauding and taking whatever tiny scraps of value might be left to them. Varvara had sought some kind of safety, although Dina didn't think her aunt truly knew—or properly bargained for—what shape that might take. Death, Dina had thought at the time, was a form of safety, yet she didn't know if the idea was hers or the Baba's.

But there was a greater price to be paid than just the body of a sick girl, of course there was. Though the crops began to revive, the sickness kept eating away at the Valley folk, and by the time they realised it, the old woman was dead and gone, beyond any kind of retribution. Soon Varvara was gone too, wondering with her last breath what she'd done. Ultimately, it took them all.

All except Dina, the girl with the Baba's heart.

•   •   •

WHEN DINA WAS at last alone, the soldiers came. A big group that time, not just one or two strays, deserters or scouts. Whatever had been happening in the world beyond the Valley had at last seen fit to pour into it. When those men came and saw there was no one but Dina, they thought she was easy meat.

She wasn't fully healed, she was tired and hungry. But the Baba's appetites were strong and growing stronger; there was Dina's body, the Baba's heart, and a ruthless pragmatism binding them together. Her nails had grown long and sharp like the old woman's had been, so sharp that she'd sliced open Dina's chest and her own with one of those talons so Aunt Varvara could pull the heart from each and swap them over. No clever surgery necessary, the Baba's magic ensured her heart took to the new body; it didn't matter what Dina's cold organ did in the Baba's worn-out corpse.

The soldiers had thought to chase her, hunt her through the woods, but she led them a merry dance. Picked them off one by one. She drew the game out, then hung them in her larder when she'd done, knowing they'd stay fine and fresh in the cold air. What she took from those men old and young had helped to sustain her, helped to heal her, helped make the raw cut in her chest close over faster.

She knew more would come, but she knew she had some time.

Today they have come.

Dina dresses in her white gown, thinks of Aunt Varvara's kind hands pulling it together, making it so very lovely. It's not a wedding dress, no, but something so much better: a coronation gown.

DINA WALKS THROUGH THE FOREST, beneath the trees festooned with crimson flesh and white bones. The red drip-drops onto her snowy dress, hitting with strange precision only the embroidered silken flowers, so it appears as though they are blossoming on the skirt, the bodice, the sleeves.

The blood from the soldiers who came before—blood that should not run any longer—liquefies and falls like a benediction. It makes a *plink* as it hits, softer on the fabric than on skin or rock, or the puddles of water where the winter fall has melted. It's not the only sound. Behind her comes the cacophony of more men, more soldiers, many more than last time. She's not strong enough to face them all, not yet, but she's cunning and she's fast; she knows these trails better than any living being. She'll leave them far behind, find the spot deep in the Red Forest where a tiny house waits, made of wood, its legs those of chickens so it can rise and walk if required. She'll know it—if the chicken legs aren't enough—by the skulls that hang on its porch, their eyes bright with flame as they watch who comes, and scream warnings to Baba Yaga.

The mortar and pestle are just down this path, hidden, waiting. She'll hike up her skirts and climb aboard, take hold of the pestle in her thin, strong hands. The vessel-vehicle will know which way to go.

Dina will warm her new home, kindle fire in its hearth. She'll rest, grow strong, become better acquainted with who she is now, with both of her selves. Then, when she is ready, she'll venture out. She'll find more soldiers and others like them. She'll find all she needs, out in the world that's just waiting for a new god.

The Song of Sighs

I

FEBRUARY *12TH*

The song of Sighs, which is his.
Let him kiss me with his mouths:
for his love is better than ichor.

THE TRANSLATION IS COMING ALONG, but
ponderously.

It takes so long to get the languages to agree, the tongues
to collude. But it is close. Some days, though, I wonder why I
don't adopt an easier hobby, like knitting or understanding
string theory. I tap on the thick folio with nails marred by
chipped polish. I remind myself this is for fun and stare at
the creamy slab of bound pages, let my eyes lose focus so all
the notations of my pen look like so many chicken scratches.
So they all cease to make sense. If I stare long enough,
perhaps I might see through time, see the one who wrote *this*
and ask, perhaps, for its greater meaning.

A polite cough interrupts my reverie. I look up and find twenty pairs of eyes fixed upon me. I realise that I heard the buzzer a full minute ago, that my class has quietly packed up their texts and pads, pens and pencils.

'Doctor Croftmarsh?' says one of them, a handsome manly boy, tall for his age, dreamy blue eyes. I cannot remember his name. 'Doctor, may we go? Only, Master Thackeray gets annoyed when we're late.'

I nod, pick his name from the air. 'Yes, Stephen, sorry. Offer my apologies to the master and tell him I will make amends. Read chapter seven of the Roux; we will discuss what he says about Gilgamesh tomorrow.'

Thackeray will expect expensive whisky in recompense; he does not miss an opportunity to drink on another's tab. His forgiveness is dearly bought, but it is easier to keep him sweet than make an enemy of him. There is the scrape and squawk of chair legs dragged across wooden floorboards, and desk lids clatter as students check they've not forgotten anything.

As they file out, I offer an afterthought: 'Those of you wishing to do some extra study for next week's exams, don't forget your translations. The usual time.'

'Yes, Doctor Croftmarsh,' comes the chorus. There will be at least six of them, the brightest, the most ambitious, those desiring ever so ardently to get ahead. This is what the academy specialises in, propelling orphans *upward*. Idly, I make a bet with myself: Tilly Sanderson will be the first to knock at 6:30.

The door closes softly behind the last of the students and the space is silent, properly silent for the first time today, no *whoosh* of breath in and out, no nasal snorts or adenoidal whistles, no sneezes, no sighs, no surreptitious farts, no whispered conversations they think I cannot hear simply because they don't want me to. Dust specks cartwheel in the shafts of light coming through the windows. I close my eyes, enjoying the sensation of not being scrutinised for however brief a time. A band of tension is tightening across my forehead. Beneath my fingers, the substantial cushion of journal pages is strangely warm.

II

February 13th
  Because of thy savour
  thy name is as fear poured forth,
  And thus do virgins fear thee.

THE REFECTORY IS awash with polite noise: the clatter of cutlery against crockery, the *ting* of glasses and water jugs meeting. Students and teachers, all at their allotted tables, talk quietly to one another, all in their own class groups.

The academy is a large place, a great building in the Gothic style: four long wings joined to make a square, with a broad green quadrangle in the middle. Two sides of the structure face the sea, looking out over the epic cliff drop; the other two are embraced by the woods and the well-tended grounds. The nearest town is ten miles distant. There is a teaching staff of twenty, three cooks, four cleaners, two gardeners, and a cadre of two hundred-odd students.

As a child, I was occasionally sent to stay with an acquaintance of my parents, here in this very house, before its owners' dipping fortunes made a change of hands essential, and it became a school for exceptional orphans. I recollect very little about those visits, having but dim impressions of many rooms, large and dust-filled, corridors long and portrait-lined, and bedchambers stuffed with canopied beds, elaborate dressers and wardrobes that loomed towards one in the night like trolls creeping from beneath bridges. I remember waking from nightmares of the place, begging my mother and father not to be sent there again.

It was only after they were gone, when I was grown and qualified, seeking employment and a quiet retreat after the accident, that I saw an advertisement for a history teacher. It seemed like the perfect opportunity. I have been here for a year.

This is what I'm told I remember.

I'm assured it's one of those things, this kind of amnesia that takes away some recollections and leaves others—I retain everything I must know in order to teach. I keep every bit of study I ever undertook tucked under my intellectual belt. I memorised the things that have happened since I came here. I may even recall the car accident—or at least, I have a sense of an explosion, of flying through the air, of terrible, intense pain—but I'm never quite sure what I can actually *invoke* of that time.

I suppose I am fortunate to be alive when my parents are not. I've been promised that many people I once knew are dead, but I'm uncertain whether I actually *feel* a loss. There are no remnants of that old life, no photos of my parents and I. No holiday snaps, no foolish playing-around-in-the-backyard photos. I have no box of mementoes, no inherited jewellery, no ancient teddy bear with its fur loved off. Nothing that might provide proof of my growing up, of my youth, of my *being*.

I fear I have no true memory of who I am.

In the same notebook where I make my translations, in the very back pages, are the scribbles I write to remind myself of who I am supposed to be. I read them over and again: I am Vivienne Croftmarsh. I have a Ph.D. I teach at the academy. I am an only child and now an orphan. I translate ancient poetry as a pastime.

This is who I am.

This is what I tell myself.

But I cannot shake the feeling that something is working loose, that the world around me is softening, developing cracks, threatening to crumble. I can't say why. I cannot deny a sense of formless dread. My hands are beginning to ache; I rub at the slight webbing between the fingers, massaging the tenderness there.

'Wake up, dreamy-drawers.' Fenella Burrows is the closest thing I have to a friend here; she plants herself and her lunch tray across from me at the deserted end of the table I've chosen. Most of the faculty take the hint and stay away, but not her and I don't mind. She tells me we went to school together, but isn't offended when I am unable to reminisce. She jerks her head towards the journal and my ink-stained fingers. 'How's it going?'

'Getting there. Second verse.'

'Second verse, same as the first,' she snorts. Fenella throws back her head when she laughs, all the mouse-brown curls tumbling down her back like a waterfall. She leans in close and says, 'Don't look now, but Thackeray is watching you.'

I pull a face, don't turn my head. 'Thackeray's always watching.'

'Oh, don't tell me you don't think he's attractive.'

Yes, he is attractive, but he stares too much, seems to see too much, seems to dig beneath my skin with his gaze and pull out secrets I didn't know were there. That's the sense I get anyway, but I don't tell Fenella because it sounds stupid and *she* clearly finds him appealing. Her smile is limned with the pale green of jealousy. 'He's all yours,' I say.

She sighs. 'If only. No one wants the plain bridesmaid.'

'How were your classes this morning?' I ask.

'Tilly Sanderson out-Frenched me.'

'That sounds appalling and punishable by a jail term.'

'Grammar-wise, you fool.' She adds more salt to the unidentifiable vegetarian mush on her plate. I can't really bear to look at it. Fenella insists it's an essential tool in her diet plan. I see no evidence: her face is still as round as a pudding and so is she.

'Well, she's very smart.'

'Yes, but I hate it when the little beasts are smarter than us.' She shovels the mess from her plate to her mouth and seems to chew for a long time.

'Honestly, don't you think eating is meant to be, if not fun, then at least easy? How much mastication does that require?'

'It's good for you; it's just a bit … fibrous.'

'It looks like the wrong end of the digestion process.'

'You're an unpleasant creature. Don't know why I talk to you.' She steals a chip off my plate.

I stare up at the head table, frown. 'Have you seen the principal lately?'

'A day or so ago,' she says. 'Why?'

'Just feel like they haven't been around for ages.'

'That'd be your dodgy memory. Old trout will be here somewhere,' she says dismissively. 'You can always talk to Candide, if it's urgent.'

'No, nothing really. Just curious. Also, I don't want to get trapped by the deputy head—last time I ended up listening to him recount his thesis from 1972 on the evils of the Paris student uprisings of '68.' Candide's about sixty, but he seems older and dustier than he should.

Fenella hooks her thumbs under the front facing of her academic gown, tucks her chin into her neck and looks down her nose at me, adopting a sonorous intonation. '"Bloody peasants, disrespecting their betters. It's all one can expect from a nation that murdered its own royalty and has far too many varieties of cheese."'

'Don't make the mistake of mentioning Charles I and the thud his head made on the scaffolding. I learned that the hard way.'

We laugh until we're gasping, and the older teachers are looking at us disapprovingly. We'll be spoken to later about the dangers of hilarity in front of the students and letting our dignity visibly slip. Causes the natives to become restless if they think we're human and we lose our grip on the moral high ground.

III

February 14th

> *Lead me, I will wait for thee:*
> *the King once summoned me into his chambers:*
> *and I was glad and rejoiced,*
> *I remember thy love more than life:*
> *All tremble before thee.*

THERE ARE two kinds of people in this world: those who, when faced with a window two floors up, will immediately accept the limitations it places upon them; and those who instantly look for a way to subvert both the height and the threatened effects of gravity. This room is full of the latter. It's one of the reasons I love teaching: the opportunity to find those who would chance a fall in the attempt to fly, rather than stay safely within bounds.

The buzz of conversation in my oak-panelled rooms washes over me. Stephen and Tilly are arguing about whether Ishtar is more or less powerful as a profligate prostitute goddess, or is simply a male wish-fulfilment fantasy; the other five watch the back-and-forth of a teen intellectual tennis match. The tipple of port has made them aggressive and I imagine sex will be the result at some point. Time to nip that in the bud. I give a slow blink, to moisten my dried eyeballs, and clap my hands.

'Enough, enough. You're not talking history anymore; you've slid into pop culture, which is Doctor Burrows' area, not mine,' I say. 'Look at the time. Off you all go.'

'Goodnight, Doctor Croftmarsh,' they say. The closing of the door and then the one student left, the one who always waits behind; the one who stands out, and frequently apart from, her fellows. Tilly, who thinks herself special, and is, I suppose. So much talent, so clever; she will do well when she goes out into the world.

'How are you?' she asks and I am a bit taken aback. She steps close, takes my hands in hers, begins stroking the palms, an intimate, invasive gesture. I don't think she knows she's doing it. 'Do you feel it yet? Has it begun?'

'Do I feel *what*, Tilly?'

Her face changes, the avid expression painted over by one of uncertainty, perhaps fear. What does the child mean?

'Tilly.' Thackeray's voice is low but seems to affect the girl like the crack of a whip. She starts and looks guilty. I didn't even hear the door open. 'Tilly, don't bother Doctor Croftmarsh. It's late and time for you to be getting back to your room.'

Tilly drops my hands and dips her head, blonde curls covering her blush-red face. She makes for the exit, then looks back over her shoulder before she leaves, smiling a sunburst at me and then throwing an odd glance at Thackeray, which I cannot interpret.

'Sleep well. Don't forget to read the Roux,' I say after her as the door closes and Thackeray leans his back against it.

He grins, his thick lips smug, then he moves into the

room without invitation and helps himself to the whisky waiting on the shelf, knocking one of the heavy crystal glasses against the other. He raises the bottle at me, and I nod. Beneath his black woollen academic robe he is still a rugby player, but slowly going soft and bloating in parts. His pale cheeks are shadowed with ebony stubble; the ruffian's posture hides an acute, albeit lazy, intelligence; sometimes I wonder how he came to teach at a place as exclusive as this.

'So, young Tilly Sanderson,' he begins, handing me one of the tumblers. His own measure is far more generous. He slumps into the chair I recently vacated, drapes himself across it, long legs stretched forward, one arm hanging down almost to the carpet, the other hand clutching his drink. His voice is low, trying for levity, but there's a dark edge that tells me to tread carefully. 'Not teaching her something new, are you?'

'Don't be ridiculous.' I sip at the whisky, feel it burn down my throat then take up residence in my belly, heating me surely as a fire. From a chest at the foot of my writing desk, I pull an unopened bottle and hold it out to him.

'What? Can't want me gone so soon, surely.' But he gets to his feet and reaches out. He wraps his large hand around not just the neck, but my hand as well, trapping me unless I want to sacrifice forty-year-old Scotch. His breath is hot and malt-rich on my face; I can feel the warmth radiating off his body, and my cheeks flame with a dim memory of drunken fumbling. I'm not sure how far it went. 'Surely we could indulge ourselves once again … Who's to know?'

I would know. And so would he. And it would give him something else to use against me in a school where fraternisation of any kind is reason for dismissal. I know how the world works; he would receive a slap on the wrist and I would be gone without references. 'Good night, Thackeray.'

I pull away and he has to juggle to save his prize. He gives a slow smile, takes his defeat well, throws back the amber in his glass, and returns the empty to the shelf.

He leaves and I feel as if I can breathe for the first time in an age. From the corridor, I hear the whisper and scuffle of boots. My heart clenches at the idea that any of the other teachers might have seen him coming out of my room. I creep over and crack the door, putting my eye to the sliver.

Thackeray and Tilly stand close, oh so close. His free hand is roaming up one thigh, over her hip, then cupping her backside roughly. Her face is hidden from me, pressed into his chest.

I step back. The headache that's been with me all day worsens; I feel as if the bones of my skull are pushing against each other. I rub my palms across my face, hoping to hold the pieces in place, to press the pain back.

IV

February 15th
  I am hidden, but lovely, O ye daughters of darkness,
  as the dreams of Great Old Ones,
  as the drowned houses of R'lyeth.

THE OFFICE DOOR, with its frosted glass panel reading simply *Principal*, is unlocked, and there is no sign of the watchdog, Mrs Kilkivan. The Tilly-Thackeray situation gave me a restless night and I thought I might approach the head before class.

Inside, the floor is covered with an enormous rug that stretches almost to the boundaries of the enormous office. The walls are covered by bookshelves, neatly stacked with hardbacks, decorative spines showing off silver lettering. Three display cases take up one corner, each with a series of ancient gold jewellery, marked with carefully handwritten labels and histories: this one found in ancient Babylon, this one from a well in Kish, yet another dug up from the depths of Nineveh, this from Ashur, these from Ur and Ebla. Artefacts excavated from the cradle of civilisation; I seem to recall the head had been active in archaeological digs in early life, and that father and mother, uncles and aunts, had all spent time in the Middle East.

Beneath the broad tall window is a desk roughly the width of the office, with just enough space to walk around, if you've slim hips. The desk is neat and tidy, a notepad on the blotter which is perfectly aligned with the edge of the mahogany edifice, the bases of the two banker's lamps also carefully placed, one on the left corner, the other one the right. The pens, fine things, are in individual cases on the polished surface; a sturdy pewter letter opener lies next to them, protected in a bronze enamelled sheath.

Some of the shelves are bereft of books, but stand instead as habitations for busts of Greek and Roman philosophers, statuettes of gods and demons, strange twisted things that would not be out of place in a museum.

Unable to resist the impulse, I step around the desk, plant myself in the ample leather seat, and try one of the drawers. Locked. All of them. I rub at my forearms; the skin is dry, thickening, irritated. The grandfather clock strikes the hour and I will be late for class. I snatch a piece of paper from the notebook and scribble a message to the principal that I need a word. I place it in the centre of the blotter, where it cannot be missed. I carefully put the pen back in its case, only after trying to wipe off any finger marks.

Here is my problem: Tilly seemed willing. She is almost eighteen—yes, we keep them here longer, if they wish. Eighteen, nineteen, twenty. Some stay on and become staff, studying, learning from the teachers here, which gives them a far better training than they would find elsewhere. Here is my other problem: the possibility of Thackeray revealing what may have happened between us, but which I am unsure even took place. And Tilly, she is a child, easily influenced.

Who do I protect? Myself or the child?

I don't know what I will tell the head. Candide will be useless; he will simply give me a slow blink and ask, *Whatever do you mean?* The principal is the key. When we meet I will know what to say.

V

February 16th

> *Look not upon me, because I am disguised,*
> *because the sun hath burned me:*
> *Earth's children were angry with me;*
> *they stole what was mine;*
> *They kept him from me.*

THE WEST WING houses the library; it's stacked with shelving and desks overrun by computer terminals and printers. A wooden set of card index drawers stands lonely and lost in the middle of the room—the young librarian doesn't know quite what to do with it and is too afraid of the ghosts of librarians past to throw it out. Curiosities abound: a giraffe's skeleton, a giant cephalopod, spears and shields and helmets of disappeared empires, bronze horse statuettes, elephant tusks, and rhinoceros horns all take up space on walls, shelves, nooks, and alcoves. There are portraits too: long-dead educators staring down with what might be disapproval or hauteur or both.

The only wall unencumbered by shelves or display items is covered by a tapestry. A woman sits enthroned on a stone seat, a staff in one hand, a snake in the other. Her eyes are wide—almost too much so, ichthyoid and protuberant—her lips pouting, her nose somewhat flat, hair a mess of black. Yet there is a kind of beauty to her, a compelling strangeness that draws the observer in. She wears a simple green robe, something that seems almost armoured, perhaps scaled, and at her slippered feet, a field of blossoms: black, silver, red, yellow, and richest chestnut petals on stalks of green. She sits most closely to the left of the tapestry—or rather, to the right —and to the right, or rather her left, nothing more than a verdant tangle of forest. Branches and trunks, undergrowth and vines, all twist together to form a dense curtain, seemingly without uniformity or plan, utterly wild and overgrown, curled around the stony ruins of a building crushed by the foliage.

In a quiet corner of the room sits Fenella, surrounded and almost concealed by a fortress of books built on the desk in front of her. At one of the tables are Tilly and Stephen and their various acolytes; I note the blonde curly head turn towards me, offering a smile, but I pretend not to see her, keep myself aimed directly at my friend.

'Have you seen the head?' I ask, *sotto voce*, as I scratch at the sides of my throat, trying to get rid of the terrible itching there. Fenella jumps, pulled from her concentration by my question, both hands thumping on the tabletop in fright.

'Don't you knock?' One of the book towers wobbles and begins a slow slide. She tries to stop it, then gives up and lets the tomes fan out, domino-like, until the final one teeters on the edge and falls. It marks the end of its descent with a noise like a shot that stops the library for a few moments.

Fenella folds her arms and looks at me.

I ask again, 'Have you seen the head?'

'This morning,' she says. 'What is *wrong* with you?'

And she's right: I'm jumpy, sweating, twitching at the slightest noise, the tiniest hints of something moving in the corner of my eye. There's still the headache: as if someone is trying to crack my skull open. And I cannot shake the accompanying sense that success will result in a dark river, a black tide flowing out of me. I blink, hard, eyes dry.

'I don't feel well,' I say. 'And . . .'

She puts a hand on my forehead—the cool flesh is a shock against my hot skin. 'Go and lie down. You don't have any classes this afternoon.'

'Thackeray,' I say, the words becoming harder to force out, the hurt pressing in on my head. 'Thackeray and Tilly, were . . .'

She tilts. The whole room tilts and I can't figure out why. I wonder that the books aren't falling from the shelves, then I realise I'm the one who's on an angle. I'm the one who's falling. I hit the floor, head bouncing against the polished parquetry.

There's a burble of noise around me. I see figures looming above, blurring. Beneath my head, I feel a beat. A thudding, ever so gentle, a mere echo of a vibration, a rhythm, a pulse, a song, but it will grow stronger, of that I have no doubt. It travels up me like a tremor, a whisper of motion. It moves me and shakes me and lulls me all at once. I close my eyes, for I have no choice, and everything is blocked out.

The last thing I hear is Fenella swearing at the crowd to stand back and let me have some air. I try to smile, but cannot feel my face.

VI

February 17th

Tell me, O thou whom my soul loveth, where thou waitest,
where thou sleepest:
for I shall not be as one turned aside
by the rise and fall of eons.

SOUND, unclear, as if heard through water. I swim up, slowly, ignoring the yearning pain in my bones. Voices. Its voices: male and female.

All I can feel beneath me now are the soft crisp linens of my bed; no more subtle rhythm, no more gentle beat. Clear-headed at last, but I keep my eyes closed, for they still retain an echo of the ache. And I listen.

'How is she?' Thackeray, subdued.

'The same as she always is at this point.' Fenella, cool. They've been arguing.

'No. It seems different—she's never struggled like this.'

Fenella is silent.

'What if she's—?'

'You're an idiot.' Fenella, angry. '*She* saw you. You can't just fuck about for the better part of a year. You put us all in danger. We're not completely invisible here.'

'We've been over this already. What does it matter? She'll be gone soon.'

'We go to all the trouble of choosing, of making each one think they're special.'

'So? I just made her feel a little bit extra special.'

'Everyone else here is *careful*. Goes out of their way to keep us all secret and safe.' Her voice drops. 'I will tell her, when this one is gone and *she's* back.'

'You worry too much, Burrows. Her time is short,' he sneers.

'She won't need long.'

That shuts him up, then there is a shuffling, his heavy steps moving away, the door opening and closing. I crack an eyelid and see Fenella, hands over her face, shoulders slumped. I know my vision is still wrong because she seems to have only three fingers. She sighs, throws back her shoulders, takes a deep breath. I focus.

She leans over me without really looking at me, touches my face. Five digits, of course; stupidity. I do not react, keep my breathing steady, slow. She steps away and leaves the room.

I wait, counting down seconds, counting down until I feel safe. I sit up, throw back the covers, swing my legs out of bed. Through the window I can see the sky, blue-black, dotted with stars, buttoned-down with a full moon. Eleven-thirty says the bedside clock. I have slept long.

My legs tremble, I straighten. My hands spasm, the base of my skull feels ... stretched. I shake my head, leave the room, uncaring that my pink flannel pyjamas are not the best attire for sneaking through corridors.

The dust and darkness are heavy in the principal's office. The moonlight streams in and on the broad expanse of the desk I can see a piece of paper. My note. Untouched, unmoved, unread.

Once again, I pull at the drawers, knowing they'll still be locked. I take the letter opener from its place and jam it into the keyhole, then into the thin space between the bottom of one drawer and the top of another, jiggle it, jemmy it, and to my surprise the bottom one grinds open with a protest. The fine dark wood splinters, exposing its pale naked inside. The drawer slides on reluctant runners.

In the bottom is a sewing-box, a padded embroidered thing, quite large, a silver toggle slid through the loop on the front to keep it closed. I unclasp it and flip it open. Inside, threads. So many threads, all twisted into figures of eight, their middles cinched in by the end of the very same thread. Tens, twenties, fifties, hundreds? So many: black, silver, red, yellow, richest chestnut. On the padded silk inside the lid, an array of needles, sentinels pinned through the fabric, all fine and golden, some thicker than others, fit for all manner of work, for varying thicknesses of material, canvas, skin, hide, what-have-you. I reach in, prick my index finger, watch the blood well and drip onto the pale blue silk, clotting bundles of thread.

I suck on the injured digit and notice, behind the casket, a creamy wad of pages. I draw them forth. Each one has a ragged edge as if torn from a journal. Each one is filled with scribbles, ancient cuneiforms of text, amateurish translations beside those obtuse scratchings:

I am hidden, but lovely, O ye daughters of darkness. They kept him from me. I remember thy love more than life. Let him kiss me with his mouths. Thy name is as fear poured forth. Lead me, I will wait for thee.

Each page dated; I can see a series of different years. How many? Oh, god, how many?

The grandfather clock interrupts me as I kneel there on the floor. It chimes the quarter-hour and I watch the hands move. The office door opens and Tilly's soft voice, rich with anticipation, a little fear, calls, 'Doctor Croftmarsh? It's time.'

'Tilly. Tilly, you have to get away from here.' I scramble up off my knees, try to move towards her at the same time, stumble twice before I stand and manage to get a hand on her arm. The touch is as much to steady me as to underline my point to her. 'There's something going on. We have to go. We'll go out through the kitchens. No one will see us—'

'Doctor Croftmarsh, don't be ridiculous,' she says, barely

concealing disdain. I tighten my fingers around her wrist. She jerks her arm away.

'No, Tilly, I'm not being silly. Something is happening and you're in danger.'

'No,' she says, smiling, but I can't quite fathom the demeanour. 'I'm not in danger—*He* has called my name and I will heed him. He will know me and choose me for I am *new*.'

And all at once I know that inimitable combination of tone and expression: triumph and malice, jealousy and hope. The child thinks she is part of a greater mystery. She thinks Thackeray will—will what? Despair and desperation well up inside me as rhythmic pulses of pain.

We stare at each other, time seemingly marching in place until, at last, there is the sound of the final *flick* of the clock hands shifting into place. Mechanisms begin to sing *midnight* and all of my agonies fall away. I smile at the girl and offer my hand in conciliation.

VII

February 18th

> *If thou know not, O thou greatest among beasts,*
> *Send me dreams so I might guess,*
> *and kill the flock by the shepherds' tents.*

WITH MY FREE hand I hook the edge of the tapestry and pull. The right half of it hangs from a rail separate to that for the left, so, when drawn across, the picture changes, the forest folded back upon itself becomes a creature, muscular, tentacled, winged; the broken stones become a second throne and the lord's limbs, now seen true, caress his bride in lewd love.

More importantly, this redecoration shows a door in the wall behind the arras, a door which leads down to the academy's rarely used chapel—to the undercroft, more precisely. I wrench it open and a whiff of dust puffs out. Dust and something else, like long-dead fish.

'Come, Tilly,' I say. There is no answer. I turn to look at her; she is staring at the hanging. I take her face in my hands, run my fingers through her hair, tender as a mother. I kiss her on the forehead, a chaste embrace, and say, 'You were right: you have been called, Tilly, and you are needed. You are anointed, the *coming one*. And *He* will know your name and I shall see you covered in the throes of glory before this night is out.'

In the darkness, I can see with the unerring gaze of a creature from the deep. In her gaze is my reflection, my features rewritten by my memories, my *true* memories: eyes set wide and angled up, ichthyoid and protuberant, pouting lips, flattened nose. And the hair, a waving tangle of green-black tentacles, ashiver with a life of their own. I stretch, my bones cracking. I am taller.

The girl's expression is stunned. 'Doctor Croftmarsh?'

I nod and smile, my teeth sharp and liberally spaced. The girl shudders. Some panic at this moment, the imminence of death shaking them from the enchantment of being chosen; some go quietly. Tilly, I suspect, is beginning to realise that she did not take note of the fine print in the deal that was struck. I lock a webbed hand around her wrist and pull her towards her destiny.

My head is full of things long forgotten, long set aside so that I—we—might hide and survive. Today, this anniversary of the Fall of Innsmouth, of my Lord's terrible injuries and afflictions, of his ever-dying, this day the memories are whole. They do not *afflict* me. They are *mine* and they rest easy in the pan of my skull.

'Never fear, Tilly.' The language feels strange in my mouth, the words seemingly square, not sibilant, not long and serpentine, but blocky. I persist, dragging the girl behind me, down into the darkness of the cold stone staircase and the crushing blackness of the undercroft and the tomb. The space is just large enough to fit the rest of the staff, teaching and domestic, all changed, all remade like me; all clustered in a tenebrous group at the far end of the crypt. 'Know that you are a part of something great.'

Here she will breathe her last, her soul, her blood given so that my lord may heal. A process oh-so-slow, but only on this one day is the barrier between his death and my life thin enough for this service.

In my haste I am clumsy.

In her terror she is strong.

When she kicks at me, I loosen my grip and she pulls away, races in the shadows, back towards the stairs, towards freedom. All the trouble gone to, to cut her from the herd, to groom her, to make her feel special—and she runs. There is the sound of a slap, a grunt.

'Careless,' says Thackeray. 'You are not what you were.' He holds the girl still, carries her as a child does a reluctant cat, her back against his chest, her limbs splayed, belly exposed. She no longer struggles. Thackeray offers her to me. I stare into her moon-wide eyes and whisper, 'All will be well.'

The talons of my right hand open up her chest, the nightgown, then the skin. A silver mist bursts from the hole, followed by a gush of blood, and both are drawn down to the stone of the tomb, then immediately begin to seep through the porous surface.

I hear, as her life pours out, the great booming rhythm of

my lord's heart, strengthened across aeons, across life and death and the space in between. Such a slow healing.

From the gloom steps Fenella, a broad smile on her plain face. 'We must talk, before you grow forgetful again,' she says.

I don't answer, merely look at the shell of Tilly Sanderson sprawled across my husband's resting place where Thackeray discarded her. The rhythm of his renewal is loud and I think: *If one can do this, then surely a legion . . .*

'You will lose yourself once more,' Fenella continues. 'We must discuss matters for the coming year.'

'Tomorrow's forgetting will be but a dream,' I say, skittering my nails across the top of my lord's tomb, finding not a skerrick of blood left there.

I am so tired of waiting.

How many years between Innsmouth and now? How many times have I taken filaments from young heads and selected a fine needle so I may embroider a new flower into the weave of the tapestry, its border growing with each passing sacrifice? How many years have I sat beside a *rock* and told my lord, my liege, my love the same tale, of the patient queen who hides away, protecting her beloved from his enemies? The tale of a wife who loses herself for his very sake, who folds the cloak of Vivienne Croftmarsh around her recollections, her histories, and suppresses everything she is so hunters may not track him through the power of her memory. A woman who sings him his song, his hymn, his dirge, and waits and waits and waits.

A woman who is weary of waiting.

From beneath, from across, I hear him sigh.

'Bring them,' I say to Burrows and Thackeray, who give me blank stares. My voice is thunder when next I speak, and they cringe with the power of my rage. 'Bring them all!'

'But—' begins Thackeray and I grab the front of his shirt

and lift him off his feet, revelling in the strength of my arm, myself; and knowing, at last, that I am unwilling to once again give up this self. I shake him for good measure.

'Bring them, by twos and threes. Bring them here and we shall see my lord awake before too many more cycles have passed. I am tired of waiting.'

A new tomorrow is about to dawn on the Esoteric Order's Orphans Academy. And then, when my lord shall finally rise again, I shall take my proper place at *His* side.

The Dead Ones Don't Hurt You

THE BRUISES WERE FADING, pale yellow with just a hint of purple now.

There was the cut above her eye, still two stitches there holding the edges of the incision together. She would have a scar. Well, it wasn't her first; wouldn't be her last.

No, she corrected herself, *that was a negative thought*. She was *not* going to think like that anymore. No more scars. No more bad boys. No more putting herself last.

Melanie smiled at her reflection, careful not to smile so much that the chipped incisor showed. (That was a remnant from Joel.) Her hair was newly bleached, a sharp platinum; her eyes were small but a bright blue. Her best feature, Momma used to say. Unfortunately she'd generally follow up with comments about pug nose, thin lips, and flat face. Melanie shook her head until her mother's voice fell away. She knew it wouldn't matter to *him*, but she wanted to wait before he saw her. First impressions and all.

The box was still where the deliverymen had left it, in that little tiny space she liked to call the entry hall. She *so* wanted to open it but she was practising patience. When she finally did, she reminded herself, she wanted to look her best.

So, she wasn't going to open the box, no. But she could do some light reading. First, there was the magazine on her bedside table. The advert was in the back, right below the singles section. When she'd seen it her heart had done little jig.

Life had seemed so empty again for a while—Cameron hadn't stayed that long. He'd gotten parole, spent two months eating her out of house and home, and then taken off, leaving her with the souvenirs of his visit on her face. She'd been wondering what she was going to do, and there was the answer, just as neat as you please, in that magazine.

Given up on live ones? For 53 payments of $29.95 per calendar month an Ever-faithful Zombie Boyfriend™ can be yours. Remember: the dead ones don't hurt you.

Then there was the owner's manual, which was even more promising:

Congratulations on choosing an EZ-Boy! Average guys too boring? Jailbirds too unpredictable? You have joined the growing ranks of women seeking a life-partner among the Walking Dead. Please read this instruction manual carefully. Failure to properly care for your purchase will render your warranty null and void. Remember: a cared-for EZ-Boy means a cared-for owner.

Life was looking up. She smeared a layer of makeup across her skin, making it extra thick over the bruises, and began getting ready for work. She was on reception at 9:00 pm.

SHAPED LIKED A COFFIN, the box kind of creeped her out. Then again, Melanie reminded herself, she had just purchased a zombie as a life-partner, so she'd best get over the squeamish. She picked up the crowbar and began the process of popping the top.

It wasn't like she'd just bought a toaster or a TV, or something you could figure out as you went along, so she'd read the manual from cover to cover. No, this was an investment in her future. Now, as she pried open the coffin, the wood splintering along the edges like toothpicks, she felt anticipation zipping around her stomach like bees buzzing in a hive, busy and warm.

She flipped the lid onto the floor and looked inside.

Well, he was handsome for sure. He looked like he might be tall too (she *had* ordered a tall one, after all). He'd short dark hair and she guessed his eyes had been blue once. Now they were kind of pearly, what with the whole patina of death thing he had going. His skin was a little grey—quite grey, actually—and yes, there was a kind of funny smell coming off him, like mothballs and something else. But he was smiling up at her like she was the moon. No man had ever looked at her like that before.

MELANIE SAT in the banana lounge on the back patio. She settled her hat firmly on her head and perched her sunglasses on her nose. Her tall glass sat on the armrest, a small circle of condensation collected at its base. Billy (that was the name she'd chosen for him) was mowing the lawn, pushing the old push mower around the yard, moving with a slight limp. She thought it might be a leftover from his life—his *living* life. He had no shirt on, six-pack in evidence, but showed no sign of sweat that she could see. One of the advantages of being a zombie, she guessed. She smiled at him and he waved and smiled back, mechanically, but nevertheless he acknowledged her and that was enough.

When she was working at the resort and if she didn't have

any chores for him, Melanie just told Billy to stay in his box. She didn't think he slept or anything; he just kind of powered down like the computers at work when no one used them for a while. He didn't really have any hobbies; it wasn't like he was going to be a big reader or need time to finish his novel or anything. He cleaned the house like a dream, but how many times could anyone do that in the week? Daytime TV rotted the brain, she firmly believed, but had to admit that it probably wasn't going to trouble a zombie too much. She thought she probably could have left him some simple cooking to do, but she was wary of having him anywhere near the salt.

The manual had been very specific about that—the type was even in a bold red—*It is important that you only ever feed your EZ-Boy the approved gruel formula (recipe attached), and under no circumstances add any sort of condiment to the mix—especially not salt. This will cause your EZ-Boy to return irretrievably to its grave and we must remind you that there are no refunds.*

So, no, that wasn't a risk she was prepared to take; she was happy to do the cooking, to make sure he had his gruel. He was *hers* and she was not letting him go for anything. She was going to be very careful with their future. She made herself comfortable and opened the magazine across her knees, so she could look between the glossy pictures and her brand-new *boyfriend.*

'So, how does he, y'know, *do it?*'

It was going so well. She took Billy to parties. He didn't talk but he was attentive, smiled at her lots, listened as she prattled and filled her glass whenever it was empty. The other girls thought she was weird at first, some kind of loser who couldn't get a live one, but by the end of the night, well, that was just another story.

All those women found that their live ones had drifted away, either to watch the football, or gather around the barbeque or the pool and drink and drink and drink until they could hardly remember their own name. Why, then her girlfriends were looking at Melanie in an entirely different light. That's when conversations like this occurred.

'Well, just the way the warm ones do it! But, oh, it lasts a lot longer,' Melanie said in a confidential tone, enjoying the attention. 'And he never complains about, y'know, eating at the Y!'

Dirty giggles all round, the sort of wolfish laughter girls made when they talked about getting the kind of sex they wanted.

'And so you say they've got a payment plan?'

She was willing to bet that more than a few relationships were going to end the next day and that *Zombies Inc.* would be doing a brisk trade.

MELANIE HADN'T BEEN EXAGGERATING. Billy wasn't like the warm ones. He didn't seem to get tired. He didn't seem to tire of doing anything, for that matter. She wasn't sure what he got out of their encounters, because he *always* had that slight smile on his face. And he never, well, *came*—just, well, kind of deflated a while after they stopped. He just kept going until she said stop. If she didn't take charge, why, chance was he'd rub her raw. After she showed him what to do it was all good.

She found, for the first time in her life, that she was the boss in the bed. He did whatever she wanted. Sometimes, she got brave and experimented. Sometimes she made him be the girl—hell, it didn't hurt *him* and she started to understand some why men had done the things they'd done to her.

She also liked those days when she could put him in the bath and give him his weekly wash. It was just like he was her doll, so pliant, so obedient. The manual insisted he be bathed only once a week: *Any more frequent washing will cause the skin to slough off in an unsightly manner. Your EZ-Boy will have its own particular scent. Do not try to wash the scent away—you will get used to it.* And she had gotten used to it. She never thought she'd start to associate mothballs with sex, but sometimes when she opened the closet in the spare room, where she kept the winter blankets and sweaters, and she caught a whiff of the camphor she'd carefully layered there at the end of season, why she just had to call for Billy.

MELANIE FOUND she had a lot of extra time on her hands, now that she had Billy. She could send him for the groceries, but she'd had to reread the manual section on giving instruction because she wanted to get it *just* right.

Your EZ-Boy is receptive to requests of quite a complex nature, but you must be very specific about what you ask for. Loose use of colloquial language could be dangerous, for example: 'Take my hand', 'Take your hands off', or 'Keep your eye on something' could lead to an incident that may void your warranty.

She'd sent him out to do the shopping one week and then had to go to the store to find him. Melanie found him standing in front of the rows and rows of different kinds of cereal, pulling on his left earlobe that way he did sometimes. When they finally got home, she lost her temper. He couldn't show any reaction of course, no contrition, and that drove her crazy—if only he'd said sorry. If only he'd been *able* to say sorry she wouldn't have gotten quite so mad, she wouldn't have started hitting him. She wouldn't have kept hitting him until her hands hurt. That's why she stopped; her hands hurt.

Melanie looked at the list she'd given him, later, and sure enough, she'd just written 'cereal'. It was all her fault. No point apologising, really, but she didn't want him making any more stupid mistakes. She wanted him to do *exactly* what she wanted him to do.

THE WOMAN at the reception desk looked familiar. Melanie gave her a bright smile as she checked the reservation in the computer. Yes, the woman had been here a few months ago—and again a few months before that. She'd always been on her own before, but not so this time. 'Hello, Ms Donaldson. Welcome back.'

The girl next to her was tall and thin, with breasts really too big for her gaunt frame. She looked like a model, was dressed like one, except for her skin and eyes—the former a definite grey, the latter cloudy white.

'An EZ-Girl!' exclaimed Melanie before she could stop herself.

The woman's eyes lit up. 'Have you got one?'

'An EZ-Boy,' said Melanie quickly, anxious that the woman know she was *straight*. Melanie eyed the girl. There was obviously a high-end to the product, one beyond her price range—this one was *very* expensive.

Ms Donaldson followed her gaze and smiled; she ran her hand proprietorially down the girl's face, neck, collarbone, and then caressed the pneumatic-looking breasts. The expression on the beautiful, blank face did not change, but she gave a little, learned sigh. 'Aren't they just fabulous?'

'Oh, my, yes. They are just fabulous. So well behaved.'

'Oh, and reliable and tireless! I don't know how I did without Felicia.' Ms Donaldson smiled fondly, possessively.

'I've put you in your usual suite, ma'am. Roger will take

your bags. Do enjoy your stay and let us know if there's anything else we can help you with.'

'Oh, I'll be very well taken care of, thank you,' she said.

THE WASHING MACHINE was broken when Melanie got home and water had flooded the laundry. Billy was mopping it up. He'd used the machine lots of time before; she'd given him very specific instructions so she knew he hadn't done the wrong thing. He didn't deviate from his learned patterns, his accustomed rhythms, nor did he think beyond the orders given him. So, she kept her temper. They bundled up the washing into big bags—she only had one uniform left for tomorrow. The girls in the laundry at the hotel wouldn't mind if she threw a few things in with the guest loads.

HALF AN HOUR before Melanie's shift started, she and Billy waited in the alcove just off the lobby. Billy carried the bags of washing and they were waiting for the service elevator to the lower levels of the hotel. Behind them came the clip-clip of high heels and they both turned to look—nothing more than a casual curiosity on Melanie's part, and simply following a lead on Billy's.

Ms Donaldson and Felicia walked past. Ms Donaldson caught sight of Melanie and gave a conspirator's wave, smiling when she saw Billy. Felicia and Billy locked eyes, but neither Melanie nor Ms Donaldson noticed because they were too busy exchanging self-satisfied smirks.

Melanie left Billy in the laundry room. The girls were happy to let Billy sit there while the cycles went through. Melanie gave him a kiss on the forehead and went back to begin her shift.

A couple of hours later, she looked up from plugging in

reservations to find Ms Donaldson with a perplexed look on her face. 'Have you seen my girl?'

'Sorry? Felicia?'

'Who else? I left her in the suite when I went to my meeting. Now I can't find her.'

'Well, no, ma'am. I haven't seen her but I will let you know if I do. I'll ask around if you like, see if we can find her.'

'Thank you. They're not supposed to wander off on their own like that!' Donaldson turned away, her heels making angry little sounds on the marble floor.

Melanie asked some of the busboys to look for the EZ-Girl and then figured she would take a break and check on Billy. When she got to the entrance of the laundry room, though, she found Lucy and Susannah and Amelia crowded in the doorway. They were giggling quietly, craning around each other to get a good look into the room. Melanie walked up behind them, her soft-soled shoes making no sound. She peered over the shoulders of the three laundresses.

Billy was sitting exactly where she had left him. Kneeling in front of him was Felicia, her head bobbing gently up and down as if in time to music no one else could hear. Melanie wondered how long they'd been going, if the EZ-Girl had the same kind of stamina as her male counterpart. She could hear a high-pitched noise. At first she thought it was one of the machines in the laundry letting off steam, until the laundresses turned around and looked at her, their mouths Os of surprise—then she realised she was screaming.

SHE'D KEPT BILLY in his box for two whole days while she decided what to do. She'd walked through her job like a— well, like a zombie—all the while her mind was on how to deal with the situation.

Melanie hadn't told Ms Donaldson. When she got her

composure back, she just returned Felicia to the suite and said she'd found the girl wandering in the gardens. They were booked for another week, so she figured she had time to think things through.

It wasn't that Melanie *hadn't* thought about telling, but she wanted to work this out for herself. She was going to take responsibility for this situation. She wanted to protect her investment.

And there was something else. Something else she wanted but couldn't bear to examine too closely for it would interfere with her view of herself. She knew it in her heart, recognised it, but wouldn't look directly at it. She wanted revenge, but she told herself it was justice. It was her right. But she couldn't afford to lose her job.

It took her two days of lurking, hours of rereading the manual, carefully timing the calls from Ms Donaldson's suite. Melanie was practised at being invisible; she blended in like a piece of furniture that no one commented on, that everyone took for granted. So she was the perfect observer—the perfect spy, really.

She was rostered on reception with Davey, a young man with a large Adam's apple that drew the eye. Melanie caught sight of the food trolley going towards the elevators just after six. She casually picked up the pile of dry-cleaning (all of Felicia's model-wear and a couple of Ms Donaldson's suits) and gave Davey a nod. They weren't busy; this was the time when she did little tasks like this. The guests liked a personal touch.

'Hold the lift!' she sang and made it between the doors just before they shut. The room service guy gave her a big smile.

'Hey, Antonio, how are the kids?'

As she moved deeper into the elevator she seemed to trip. The dry-cleaning dropped to the floor with a whisper of plastic, individually wrapped pieces sliding over one another, slippery as squid in a bowl. Antonio bent down to pick them up. Melanie lifted the metal lid from the bowl of Felicia's gruel with her left hand and with her right dug into the pocket of her jacket and scooped out the grains of salt she'd spooned in there before the beginning of her shift. The crystals shone under the fluoro lights as she sprinkled them over the surface. They melted quickly into the beige-coloured mush, and she gently replaced the cover as Antonio stood, the dry-cleaning tidily arranged, the metal hooks of the coat hangers curved over his thick fingers.

In another day or so she'd let Billy out of his box. She'd explain to him again what he'd done wrong. She wanted him to know he could never do that again. She'd tell him what she'd done. She wanted him to know she was protecting him. Protecting her *investment*.

Sun Falls

I TAP the fingers of one hand against the steering wheel, beating out a rhythm to replace the one that went missing when we got beyond the reach of any radio reception. It helps me to ignore the noises from the backseat.

The window is down so I can blow away the smoke from a hand-rolled ciggie. Barry hates it when I smoke in his car. Few things in the world Barry loves more than this old Holden, with its mag wheels, racing stripes, flames painted on the bonnet, and the fluffy dice dangling from the rear-view mirror like a pair of square, furry testicles. He adores it better than any woman. I wouldn't be allowed to drive if it weren't an emergency of the *most* urgent kind.

Me? I think he looks like an idiot driving it, like some clueless pimp. But I'm not stupid enough to tell Barry that. Nope, not stupid enough at all. And it's not as if I'm paid for my opinion. In fact, I'm not paid. Just here to shut up and earn my keep, as Barry says. Just like my mum did before me and her mum before that, all serving Barry for as long as we can remember.

Two hundred years, give or take. It's a long time to be a slave.

Outside it's cooling down, which is a blessing because the air-con died a few hours back. The sky is splashed garish pink by the setting sun and now it's low enough to not hurt my eyes. I push the cheap sunnies to the top of my head, hook the earpieces into my hair so they stay put. I enjoy the rush of the breeze moving in and out of the car. The sounds of the night start too: cicadas, possums, snakes, lizards, hares, wallabies. All manner of nasties that don't come out in the sunlight.

Kinda like Barry.

I can't hear the words he's shouting, but he knows the dark's come and he wants out. I've got a fair idea what he's saying. *Terry, open the fucking box.* There'll be that for a few more k, then *Teresa, love, sweetie, please open the box. Please let me get some fresh air. It's cold in here.*

I leave it just until I sense he's about to move to threats, then I reach behind, keeping my eyes on the road, feel around on the backseat, find the cooler, and flip the lid off. It lands on the floor with the sort of noise only falling polystyrene can make, both offended and humble, a sort of squeal like it's not happy but doesn't want to bother you.

'Thank fuck for that!' Barry's got quite a voice on him for someone currently without lungs. 'Are you deaf?'

'Couldn't hear you, Barry. Engine's too noisy.' And the machine doesn't make a liar of me—it rumbles and protests like an old man with emphysema. 'It's been a long trip.'

'Well, this thing better keep going, I can't afford to get stuck out in the middle of nowhere in this state.'

Barry's 'state' has been a cause of concern for a couple of days now. There have been gang fights on the streets of Sydney—not the usual sorts, not the drug peddlers or the slave traders, not the gunrunners or the money launderers.

Not this time anyway. Rival gangs of bloodsuckers, all trying to survive, to reach the top of the tree. All trying to be the big dog and negotiate with the breeders, those few Warm who are in the know (even with the current state of societal decay, there are some things you don't want the general populace to find out). But there are those who understand the night isn't a safe place, never has been, not since the First Fleet came and nicked the nation from under the nose of the indigenous population. That even on those ships, the greatest enemy wasn't scurvy or the lash, it was the things, just one or two, that roamed the lonely hours picking off the weak so as not to draw attention to themselves. Those who slept nestled in hidden compartments until the daylight hours passed.

Barry was one of them. Nasty bastard, by all accounts (I've read the diaries my grandmothers kept). Didn't make too many of his own kind initially, just found a thin girl, none too bright, pregnant and fearful, someone he could bully and boss, someone who could do what was needed when the sun ruled the sky, who thought his protection worth the price of her liberty. Minnie: my ever-so-great-grandmother, a silly little pickpocket too slow to not get caught, who sold all our freedoms with her one stupid decision.

She couldn't read or write, but her daughter could, so Minnie told the story and her girl wrote it down. And so on and so on—we've all kept notes of some kind, some more literary than others. The Singleton women have quite a collected work now.

After Minnie's dimness, Barry decided we'd be more useful if educated, so good schools for his girls, university if you wanted it (I have a science degree, for all the good it did me). He never turned any of us, just kept us, generation after generation, like family retainers ... or pets. We don't run. I asked my mum why, but she just gave me that sleepy junkie smile. In her own way she did run—she just found her escape at the pointy end of a needle.

I've thought about it a lot in the years since and I reckon we stay put because we're told from the cradle there's nowhere else to go. How do you outrun the night? How do you go on living when closing your eyes means you might wake with a weight on your chest that doesn't go away? It's easier to live in the eye of the storm than to try and outrun it. And, ashamed as I am to say it, the protection of the devil you know is preferable to being meat to something else. There are worse things in the dark than Barry.

Of course there's always the theory that girls without fathers will attach themselves quite willingly to father figures. Barry's a bad dad if ever there was one, but he's always looked after us. Can't argue with that.

So we shut up, do what's expected, or find a way out. I'm never quite sure if Mum intended things to go the way they did. The drugs numbed her, but she could function, and Barry turned a blind eye. I guess I always thought it would go on like that forever, until I got the call to say Barry had found her one night, stiff and cold under the pergola, propped against the BBQ with the little silver happy stick still in her arm. So, the big recall for me. Goodbye, uni; goodbye, honours degree; goodbye normal life.

But I digress.

Barry and his state.

He thought himself safe, thought himself well protected. He'd built up his empire and believed himself king of the vampires. Didn't occur to him that his bodyguard—not me, I'm just a kind of housekeeper—might not be content with the status quo. That Jerzy might want a change of pace, of lifestyle, of regime. That Jerzy might take the great big Japanese sword Barry liked to keep hanging on the wall of his study and use it to separate Barry's head from the rest of his body before the other bodyguards had a chance to tear Jerzy up like a hunk of shredded pork. Then, untethered, they all bolted out of the big house with its Greek columns and stamped concrete driveway, its seldom-used-in-daytime swimming pool, blackout blinds, and luxuriously appointed cellar, leaving the wrought-iron gates open and me to wander in from the kitchen to find that all the excitement had passed.

What should I see but Barry's head still intact? His body nothing but a pile of cinders and ash, but the head was all in one piece. And talking. Well, less talking than screaming and yelling obscenities. That's when I went to find the cooler, as much ice as I could, and Barry's car keys.

And here we are, heading towards the arse-end of nowhere because Barry says so. Because he says there's a place he can find help, a place where life begins again.

THE ROAD IS MORE dirt than black stuff now and it's starting to rise, just a little. Around each bend, the incline gets steeper and the car protests more loudly. Soon, I should imagine, it will make its wishes known with the mechanical equivalent of a big *fuck you.*

'So, tell me how this is going to go again, Boss.'

Dawn is starting to grey the sky, and Barry's gotten lethargic as you might expect. He's quietened down and I should probably put the lid back on his box—the last of the ice I'd dumped in the Esky turned to warmish water hours ago, but I don't guess he'll drown. Looks like he's immortal, if not invulnerable.

'It'll all be sweet, Terry. I'll be good as new.' His voice is low and sleepy.

'Fine and dandy, Barry, but what are the details? What about me?'

'What about you? This isn't about you, you dopey bitch.' More awake now.

'Never said it was, Barry, but: point of order. We're walking into this place. What's out there? More of your brethren? You're not really in a position to protect me, are you? I'm a canapé on legs. So, *what's out there?*'

'Nah, Terry,' he says, but he doesn't sound very sure. 'It'll be okay. Nothing there, no one. Nothing to worry about.'

And for the first time in my life I don't believe Barry. I don't trust him to look after me and it gives me a funny feeling in the pit of my stomach. Of course, that could be hunger—that last apple was three hours ago, and I'm down to a packet of muesli bars and a tube of Pringles. 'Sure, Barry. Sure.'

No one, my arse. I know enough about bumps in the night and deserted dead hearts to know nothing's ever really empty. If Barry knows about this place, so does someone else. *You're not king of the vampires here, Bazza. You're just a talking head.* I pull over to the shoulder of the road, reach back, and put the lid on Barry and his polystyrene swimming pool. I get out of the car and look around, stretching my long body as my back protests and my worn-too-long cargos and tee stick to my skin. I can smell my own sweat and the determined stink of the cigarettes that ran out not far out of Sydney. I stare into the bush. It's changing as we head up the mountains, getting greener, darker, denser, wetter. More like a rainforest. Not sure what I expect to see ... Nothing there, no movement, not even the twitch of a leaf in the breeze. I feel weird, though; I feel watched. *Imagination,* I tell myself. *Bullshit,* I tell myself.

I slide back into the driver's seat and turn the key in the ignition.

The only answer I get is the exhausted metallic grinding of a thing that's gone as far as it can go. I lean forward and rest my head against the steering wheel, smelling the stale-sour scent of hands gripped too long about the leather cover. My spidey senses tell me this road trip will not end well.

I'VE GOT Barry's box in one hand and in the other is the long Japanese sword that parted him from his body. It seemed like a good idea to bring it along—just made sure Barry didn't see it, sore point and all that. The water bottle hanging at my waist is making sad little wishy-washy sounds. Not much more than a mouthful left and I'm thirsty. The need for nicotine is dancing under my skin.

The air is cool and damp, the clouds are sitting on the road, and it's hard to see too much in front of me. The condensation is plastering the fringe to my forehead. It's mid-afternoon and I don't know where I'm going; I'm just following the road. Can't open the box to ask Barry; he's been in deep sleep for hours now. I just keep walking, although my boots have rubbed blisters onto my soles and the outer edges of my little toes.

Up ahead I can hear a sound, sweet and clear. Water.

I pick up my pace and stumble off the road, down a slight slope to find a clearing, a little creek running through it. There's a fire pit that looks like it hasn't been used in a long, long time. I refill the water bottle, drink deeply, then peel off my boots and socks and plunge my feet in. It's icy and hurts only for a little while before the numbing cold makes everything seem okay. I lean back, raise my face to where the sun should be, and imagine it on my skin. Problem with being in service with a night crawler is that you don't tend to see too much daylight. Oh, you have to run errands and some of those are unavoidably day-oriented. But mostly, you become as nocturnal as your master. Feels like shift-work. Do it long enough you either get used to it or go nuts. Or a bit of both.

Behind me there's a sound—behind me, where I dropped Barry's box (the katana I kept close). There's that distinct polystyrene noise and I turn to see the biggest freaking possum I've ever seen in my life. It looks like a large dog, a Labrador maybe, on its hind legs, and it's got the lid off the cooler and one paw buried deep inside. It pulls Barry's head out by the messy black hair.

There it dangles at the end of possum claws, eyes closed, lips slack and a little open, and the neck so cleanly severed you could almost admire it as a nice tidy job. I stand slowly. The possum sniffs at Barry's nose, licks it, then opens its mouth and sinks sharp white teeth into the substance of Barry's pert little snoz.

I take a good few fast steps and bring the katana sweeping upward, and the possum paw drops to the ground, leaving Barry hanging briefly by his nose in the grip of the teeth of a very unhappy marsupial. Possum spits out its lunch and gives me a look that makes me think twice about getting any closer. Then I remember that I've got the sword and about four feet in height on the thing. But it's fast and the remaining claws sharp; my cargos and the leg underneath get a nasty gash before I manage to take the stinking thing's head off.

I have a rest, bent over, hands on knees, breathing hard while I watch blood dribble out of my injured flesh. There's a yell and I fear a possum support column may have arrived. But it's only Barry, waking up.

'What the fuck happened to my nose? Do you have any idea how much this hurts? What the hell did you do to me?'

'Oh, Barry, you don't want to know. Now, which way? There are no signs for Sun Falls.'

'Just keep following the road.' The he pitches his eyes

downwards, trying to get a good look at the state of his nose. I manage not to laugh as he goes a little cross-eyed. 'Fuck this hurts.'

A BONFIRE and five figures gathered around it: a woman, an old man, two young men, and a teenage girl. Raggedy stragglers, left out here with orders to guard the place, I guess. They're vampires, though, so it doesn't matter if there are five or a hundred. The rush and roar of water is clear from somewhere in the darkness. I can feel a damp spray I think might come from the falls.

I washed the wound and wrapped my leg up tight, but I know they can smell it before I step into the circle of light. There's a collective growl that must be something like a gazelle hears before a pride of lions brings it down. I might be able to take out a couple before they get to me. The fire catches the edge of the katana and pinwheels in Barry-unboxed's wide open eyes. The pack stays back, however. I must look as though I know what I'm doing—well, you can fool some of the vampires some of the time, I guess.

The woman stands and takes a few steps towards me.

'Hello, dinner,' she says. 'How obliging of you to turn up.'

'You might want to rethink that,' I say, and raise my boss's head.

Barry pipes up, 'Lynda, keep your hands off her. She's no one's meal.'

'Is that you, Barry?' The woman squints. Her hair is wound into filthy dreads, not all of her teeth remain, and the breeze tells me she's not washed in some time. Hillbilly vamps, who'd have thought it? Feeding on the occasional lost tourist, stray cattle, giant possums. 'Aw, Barry. What the fuck happened?'

'Long fucking story. I need to use the pool,' he says shortly.

'The pool? No one's done that in a hundred years—you dunno what's gonna happen.' She gets a cunning look in her eye. 'What's it worth to ya?'

'How about a snack?'

Told you Barry was a nasty piece of work. But you know what, I'm less afraid of him than I am of them. One thing I do know is this: no matter how much he lies to everyone else, he's always kept his word to my family. He said I would be safe. He's also the only thing protecting me from the cast of a bloodsucking *Deliverance*.

I'm flanked by two underfed youths with straggly beards and, if I didn't know better, a look that says 'Inbreeding keeps it in the family'. One of them carries a torch plucked flaming from the fire. They don't need it to see—hell, they don't need fire at all, but I recognise in the building of the bonfire a remnant of their warm days, a little thing to hang onto. A memory of way-back-when, of kids playing at grown-ups, of a time when heat meant comfort, meant life. Creatures pretending one day there might be light.

The falls are a couple of minutes' walk away, down a path strewn with sticks and pebbles, occasionally hidden by touchy-feely ferns. When we reach the bottom, there's a shallow pool and a whole lot of spray where the water crashes down. One of my escorts points to a break in the foliage, right next to the cataract; the other pushes me roughly forward. My Docs slip and slide on the damp rocks. I keep my balance, though; with a head in one hand, a sword in the other, and Barry cursing me the whole while, it's no mean feat. I walk around behind the curtain of *wet* and see an entrance, a glow coming from inside it like a jack-o'-lantern.

There are no torches here, I notice, but the walls glow.

Phosphorous? I wait until we're far enough down the tunnel for my guard of honour to not hear.

'Barry, you ungrateful bastard. I carry your sorry metaphorical arse all the way here, nearly get eaten by a mutant possum, and this is the thanks I get?' I shake him by the hair and glare into his blue eyes. 'You think I'm an hors d'oeuvre?'

'Calm down. Wait—possum? Is that what happened to my nose? You let a possum eat my fucking nose?'

'Focus, Barry. Seriously, do you think I'm going to drop you in the all-healing, all-fixing pond so you can serve me up to that lot?' I shake him again and he winces. 'Or are you gonna snack on me yourself?'

'Don't worry about it. Once I'm whole again, no one's going to mess with you.'

'You didn't answer me!'

'I might need a little blood when I'm done,' he admits. I give his head a good rattle and a few choice profanities, and he yells, 'Not much! Not much! Just a little to top up. I promise!'

'What are we talking? A thimbleful? A shot glass?'

'Just a—bit. Terry, I promise I won't drain you, I won't turn you.'

What choice do I have? The devil I know or the ones I don't.

The pool is at the bottom of the slope, in roughly the centre of a small cavern. The liquid in it is milky white, with the same sheen as mother-of-pearl, and the smell is a little like household cleaner. A bit bleachy—more Domestos than Dettol.

'What's that?' I ask, trying not to breathe too deeply.

'Stuff. You know—stuff.'

'You knew about this how?'

'Stories, Chinese whispers, old diaries—your lot aren't

the only ones who keep records, you know. Nothing precise, nothing exact, just hints.'

'You *read* our diaries?' I shouldn't be surprised.

'Yeah, yeah, yeah, I'm a bad person. Throw me in.'

'But what if it doesn't work?'

'Not really in a position to be picky, am I? Fountain of youth, a wellspring, a cauldron of plenty. There are legends and they all say it brings life.'

I don't point out to Barry that strictly speaking he has been for some time well and truly beyond the usual span of any creature. Well and truly outside the spectrum of what we call life.

'So,' I say, 'life?'

'Life. Now hurry the fuck up and toss me in.'

I walk around the edge. It's about five metres across and bubbling enthusiastically. If I drop him, maybe he'll just drown—which still leaves me with a problem.

'Here's the deal, Barry: I'll put you in but in return you let me go. I'm no one's lunch, I'm no one's slave, I'm gone. I'm out. I do whatever I want.'

'Terry . . .'

'You want life or not?'

'Yes, fuck it!' He gives a growl of frustration. 'All right. Agreed. I can find better than you at the local whorehouse anyway.'

'Touché.'

I kneel beside the pond and lower Barry in, resisting the impulse to drop him from a height to see how much of a splash he'll make. Some of the fluid leaps up like a nipping fish and lands on my fingers. It stings like ice. I grit my teeth and keep going, don't release the head until he is well and truly submerged.

I try to straighten up, withdraw my arm, but I feel sharp teeth in my wrist. Barry, you bastard. That, however, is the least of my problems: the water has me. Blood spurts from my nose and turns pink as it hits the milky pond. It's like I'm in the grip of an electrical current. It tugs at me and tugs at me until I over-balance and it pulls me beneath the surface.

I feel as if I'm dying forever.

My last sight before I'm overwhelmed is Barry's head tossed and churned, jumping about like popping corn. Angry fingers of fluid force their way into my mouth and race down my throat, filling my lungs like inhaled fire. My skin seems to peel off; each hair follicle is a tiny pin in my scalp. Surely my eyes burst.

When it stops hurting, the water lets me go.

I crawl out and lie on the surprisingly warm rock. I'm whole, intact, if somewhat soaked. I rub a hand against my shin, right where the possum bite was and feel . . .

And feel . . .

Nothing.

I roll up the leg of my cargos and strip away the bandage. There's just a pink mark that might have been a scar but fades as I watch. The katana is where I left it, and I pick it up, prick at my finger with its sharpness. Something silver oozes out from the cut and just as quickly the opening closes over.

A great spout of water comes from the pool and a body lands not far from me, gives a displeased groan.

Barry, whole again, tall and handsome and muscular and . . .

And no longer pale, as if he tries to tan beneath the moon.

He rolls on his back, coughing, making a noise like an espresso machine. He *breathes*. I poke at him with the katana. A tiny drop of blood blossoms on his skin and he swears. Rich, fresh, oxygenated, *living* blood.

'Oh, Barry,' I say. 'You were right.'

He sits up, runs his hands over his arms and legs, wondering, not understanding. 'But . . .'

'It does give life, Barry. You've been dead a long time.' I can't keep the laughter out of my voice.

'But ... Fuck!' He stands up, pacing. 'Okay. I don't have to outrun them, I just have to outrun *you*.'

'Here's the thing, Baz: I don't think they're going to be interested in me anymore.' I rise, do the thing with the poking and the quick silvery bleed. 'Close as I can figure it, nature abhors a vacuum. The pond finished what you started, taking my blood and all, then ... replaced it.'

I start up the path, cast a look behind. 'Long time since you've been meat. How's it feel?'

The Way of All Flesh

SINCE EVERYTHING WENT TO HELL, Sweet Bobby Tate had found some—indeed, all—of his preferred activities curtailed. This vexed him no end. He was fond of travel—although he could take or leave the big cities; not that there were too many of them anymore—but what he really liked, where his heart truly resided was in small towns. The smaller the better, as far as Bobby was concerned: easier to meet people, get to know folk. Faster to get around and finish the conduct of business.

In small towns, Bobby would tell anyone who stuck around long enough to hear; people did you the courtesy of conversing. Taking the time to listen. People there were trusting, and Bobby liked that too. He liked how small towns had layouts that were easy to figure, and how they almost always had pleasant and interesting graveyards. Small towns had little old churches of wood, with peeling paint, flower beds awash with colour, prayer books lined up neat and tidy, all manner of altar cloths handmade by the local ladies. There were stone walls around such boneyards, not so high that climbing over them caused a pulled muscle or torn seams in tight jeans, but high enough to give a little privacy.

Cities had less space and so leaned towards crematoria, with niches and so forth—less cadavers, more urns of ashes. While Bobby was not averse to a barbeque on occasion, he preferred things *fresh*.

Bobby's Momma had often told him, *Fresh is best* and her words were a sermon he took to heart. She didn't get out much in her later years and she hated travelling as much as her boy loved it. She looked forward to his visits, though, hearing him tell of his adventures as he crisscrossed the great nation like some latter-day Johnny Appleseed, sewing darkness wherever he went. The last time he dropped in on her—before the world had started to fall apart—he'd found her still and cold in her easy chair. No more cosy chats and homey wisdoms, no more games of cheating chess, and the loss hit Bobby hard. He was grateful it was winter and she'd not paid her heating bill.

He made himself a feast she'd have been proud of, ate every last morsel. She would have wanted it that way, he thought; hadn't she fed his infant mouth with slivers of her own flesh and quenched his thirst with her own redness? Every time he'd seen those scars on her arms, in the places where the flesh was softest, he choked up, knowing he was so loved. Whenever he came into a new town and saw a woman who reminded him of his mother, he made sure she was his very first acquaintance.

So when Sweet Bobby Tate stepped across the boundary into Wolf's Briar, West Virginia (Population: 332), footsore and hungry, the primary thing he cast around for was a bakery. On any day not Sunday, that was where you found ample women with grey hair, heavy breasts, and loose cotton shifts, smelling of lilac toilet water or lily of the valley. Later on he'd try the church.

. . .

ANNABEL ADAMS—SIXTEEN AND PRETTY, with only a slight overbite that barely anyone ever commented on anymore—sat on the porch swing and gently kept it rocking with the occasional tensing of her leg muscles. The breeze was agreeable and cool as it rustled through the branches of the old lemon tree. It hadn't brought any awful sort of smell for weeks now, so Annabel figured that whatever had been rotting in large quantities some distance from Wolf's Briar had finished its decaying. The weather was nice, almost on the turn from summer to autumn, and she thought it was her favourite time of year. Behind her, the big white house was quiet: no voices, no music radio, no hum of a refrigerator or air conditioner, coz no one had heard that for almost a year. Just as quiet as the church and god-acre next door, just as quiet as dust falling.

Annabel did a quick calculation and figured it was more than a year—closer on eighteen months. The power gave out the day before her brother Tim went the way of all flesh. Annabel didn't like to say 'died'. She hadn't thought about it too much before what her Grandma Eileen called the Great Retribution came, but when it got to the point that so many folks she'd known all her life just weren't there anymore, she decided a new term was needed. Slowly but surely, just about everyone went the way of all flesh. She was happy her family had stayed with her, though, after everything that had happened, even if they didn't say much anymore.

Sighing, she stood and the swing banged back against the wall, taking out another chip of paint. Annabel stretched, long black hair trickling down her back. Her gaze flitted over the dusty length of the street, the lonely-looking houses, and overgrown lawns, and saw what she saw every day: precisely nothing new.

'Back to the books,' she said, so her mother might hear and know she wasn't slacking. It was important, Melba Adams said, to stay up-to-date with all the subjects she'd need for her SATs, because surely one day things would get better and she'd want to go to a good school.

That was Melba's mantra: *Things will get better*. Her mother had been certain, so absolutely convinced that one day all the bad stuff would be done with. That one day the power would magically come back on, that they'd get something more from the landline than petulant silence, that their mobiles would once again start pinging signals from towers, and hallelujah, the tiny gas station at the end of Abel's Road would be pumping petrol into all the SUVs currently standing idle in people's drives. None of that happened, though Melba said they should just be grateful none of those walkers mentioned on the radio—back when the batteries still had juice and some places had generators that let them broadcast—ever came near Wolf's Briar. Annabel didn't share her mother's faith in the Restoration of Everything, but she kept up her studies for Melba's sake.

'Back to the books,' she said again, and then stepped into the cool interior of the house.

MUCH TO HIS CHAGRIN, Sweet Bobby found no trace of either portly matrons nor working bakery. Indeed, there was no trace of anyone anywhere. The shelves in the supermarket had been picked clean for the most part, except for a few unloved tins of peas, ravioli, beets, and thirty-two packs of Junior Mints.

He wondered if the dead walkers had been through, but there were none of the usual signs left when those locusts on two legs paid a visit: no empty bullet casings scattered like metallic fruit, no bodies in various stages of decay littering the streets, no houses hastily fortified and then broken open like Easter eggs. Everything was just quiet and empty and filled with different degrees of dust.

Perhaps the inhabitants of Wolf's Briar had decided to head to one of the safe zones early on—but surely they'd have taken their vehicles, as long as the gas held out? Without much hope, he decided to give the rest of the town a once-over. Who knew? He might get lucky at the cemetery, find someone buried not *too* long ago and not too deep.

He wandered up the deserted main street, past empty-eyed shops until the shops became cottages, then cottages grew into larger houses as they got closer to land that might be farmed. Soon enough he spotted it: a stone wall, not too high, not too low, the tips of grave markers peaking over the top, and the pale yellow-painted planks of a tiny church. Bobby put some pace into his step, a smile pulling up one corner of his mouth like a fishhook.

He vaulted the wall, his boots kicking up an awful lot of dust and dead grass. With a keen eye he looked over the simple headstones and the mounds in front of them, saw that most of them were sunk with age instead of reaching upwards. Some had metal grilles over them, slowly rusting. In disgust, he kicked a largish rock and heard it strike against the timber of the church. Sweet Bobby stalked along one side of the graveyard, then turned a right angle and paced the distance to the opposite wall. As he got to the next corner, he stopped.

A large white house, three storeys high, with a broad veranda. Colourful curtains fluttered in and out of windows. A place that did not look empty or deserted. And then, flitting from one set of open French doors to the next, was a girl. Thin, knobbly knees, a white-and-black polka-dot skirt, and tiny breasts under a washed-out t-shirt. She was singing to herself, off-key, some song he didn't recognise. Her voice cracked partway through the last word and it made him laugh.

He hitched the satchel firmly on his shoulder, and made a beeline for the tall house.

'Now, Daddy, don't look at me like that. I'll make him welcome.'

Her father's expression was the one she thought of as his sermon face, just like he used when in the pulpit, talking about the lack of a moral compass in their community. He'd given her the heads-up, turning his mostly-bald head towards the front door just moments before the stranger's lean shape darkened the rectangle of light. Annabel stretched away from the kitchen bench so she could see all the way down the hall and take in the visitor. She kept her breathing calm, although her heart skipped, just a little.

'Hi there,' he called. 'Mind if I come in out of this heat?'

'Of course,' she said like a polite young lady, not contradicting him about the weather coz it really was quite pleasant outside. 'Would you like some lemonade? It's from our very own lemons.'

'I did notice that tree hanging over the cemetery wall,' he called while he paused and removed his boots before crossing the threshold. Annabel took the opportunity to gather all the condiments she needed for his beverage. By the time Bobby had sock-footed it into the bright kitchen, Annabel was pouring a tall glass of lemonade from an old crystal pitcher.

'I'm Bobby Tate,' he told her—he didn't tell anyone that he was *Sweet* Bobby until the very last minute.

The girl held out the glass, rough-torn leaves of mint contrasting with the pale yellow liquid. Her hand didn't shake as their fingers brushed, and he was kind of disconcerted by that. Then, again, he thought, folks had become strange since the changes; some got friendlier, some got braver, some more easily spooked.

'I'm Annabel Adams and I'm sorry the lemonade's not so cold,' she said, sweeping her hair back from her face, carefully knotting the strands into a fat bun at the back of her head, then took up one of the pencils that lay on an open exercise book and jammed it through the thickly wound ball.

The girl smiled. 'How do you come this way, Mr Tate? Wolf's Briar's so far from anywhere.'

'Oh, I'm just a roaming soul. Besides, there's not much left out there,' he said, gesturing in the general direction of 'out there'. Bobby took a swig of the lemonade, then another —it was good, sweet. The girl busied herself tidying, lining the exercise book up with the edge of the counter, then closing the textbook next to it.

He took Annabel Adams in like a butcher assessing a calf. She hadn't been eating particularly well, but she *had* been eating. He thought about the long-bladed knife in his satchel, but decided that could wait; he liked to get up close and personal with his food first of all. This girl was slender; she wouldn't prove too much of a challenge. Bobby knew from past experience that he would prevail—it was one of the things he liked best about himself.

He put his now-empty glass gently down on the slick surface of the bench. Or he thought he did; there was a moment when it seemed settled, then it was falling, falling, and next it was in pieces on the cool floor of grey tiles. Sweet Bobby stared at the remains as they caught the last of the light from the wide window above the sink. He could have sworn he'd placed that damned cup firmly, solidly, down on the flat expanse.

The girl was unperturbed by the loss of her glassware. She smiled at him and behind her, figures started to appear. Bobby blinked hard, once, twice, trying to focus, to make those pale pasty white things *sharpen*. But they remained quite stubbornly insubstantial—almost swirly. A big-boned man, a thin woman, two young boys—maybe twins—a girl not much older than Miss Annabel here, and finally an old woman with what looked like a shawl of cobwebs thrown jauntily around her shoulders. They looked light as gossamer, pale as angels.

'Don't worry about that, and don't worry about them— although don't you think Daddy would look best with wings? Did you like the lemonade?' asked Annabel. 'Not too much sugar?

Bobby shook his head like a dullard, tried to say 'Just right', but his tongue felt thick and slow, didn't want to form words. He grunted, which the girl was too polite to comment upon.

'Coz,' she continued, 'you need the sugar to cover the taste of the powder.' She saw his expression and laughed. 'Oh, hell, it's not poison, if that's what you're thinking, Mr Tate—that would ruin the meat.' She addressed the hefty vaporous man, 'Sorry, Daddy, I didn't mean to curse, I just got carried away.'

The spectre nodded patiently. The woman beside him looked like an ageing cheerleader and pointed at Sweet Bobby.

'Yes, Mama,' she said with barely veiled impatience. 'Miz Melba May Adams, pointing, pointing, pointing, just like she did in life.' But Annabel stubbornly refused to pay attention, which was why Sweet Bobby fell so hard, hitting his head on the corner of the bench. Melba's movements headed into semaphore.

Annabel sighed and nodded. 'Yes, Mama, I should have listened to you.'

She bent over and the shades leaned forward too, so all

Bobby saw was a circle of faces, staring down with various degrees of curiosity.

'It was nice to talk to you, Mr Tate, if only for a little while. My family don't say much – well, nothing really. But I do appreciate them sticking with me even after all that happened. I left them til last, you realise, because I love them; did not touch them until no one else was left in Wolf's Briar for me to take in the night. They were kind in life, and very forgiving in death. They gave up the ghost for me, so I could keep my strength until things get better.'

Bobby's eyes drooped and drooped.

'That's the temazepam, it's a hypnotic to send you off to dreamland. Tastes awful bitter, though—that's why the lemonade needs so much sweetening.'

Bobby tried to talk, although what he might have said he wasn't certain. He might have cursed, or maybe offered his admiration for a game well played. He thought he might have said, *You're the girl I always dreamed of.* The light from the window was dimming, the dusk creeping in like a heavy secret.

'Don't you worry, Mr Tate. You won't even know what happens to you, and I won't be so cruel as to tell you. You'll sleep forever—' she broke off, distracted by the waving of her father's head, then nodded. 'You'll sleep like an innocent baby taken up to paradise. Now, isn't that the best gift anyone's ever given you?'

She smiled and as he drifted off, Bobby heard Annabel Adams's final words on the matter: 'He shouldn't have thrown that rock and made all that noise.'

Her family nodded in agreement.

'Nice round buttocks, juicy and firm. He'll keep in the cellar with some salting and drying. I'll get a year off him if I'm not greedy—yes, Daddy, I learned that lesson. Going to be heavy, though; pity none of you have the wherewithal to help me.'

And because the words had lost all meaning for him, they sounded, to Bobby's drowsing ear, like the sweetest lullaby in the world.

The October Widow

Mirabel Morgan suspected herself hunted,
though she'd caught no trace of whoever was pursuing her.

She was careful when she left the house, keeping a
weather eye on the rear-view mirror, but able to discern no
particular vehicle standing out from those sharing the road
with her. At night, she made sure to close the curtains well
before darkness fell, when lights might pick her out as a
target against the evening gloom. Yet no one appeared on the
pavement or stoop. There were no raps at the door, no
envelopes in the mailbox. No sign that she should flee. She
watched the calendar tick over with inexorable certainty, and
as the day paced closer, the grid of nerves inside her chest
tightened like wires pulled by circus strongmen.

Tendrils of white had appeared at her temples regular as
clockwork, and her face, though still handsome, had crow's-
feet radiating from the corners of her eyes, and lines formed
parentheses from nose to mouth. The chin was less firm than
it had been, but her cheekbones still soared high, kept her
profile patrician. Her knuckles were swollen, like dough sewn
with yeast and carelessly kneaded, furrows left embedded.

They'd been aching since the temperatures had lowered, the same gnawing pain that afflicted her at this time. Made it harder to do things when she most needed to be agile, if not sprightly. Every cycle she told herself that the next would be different, that she'd be better prepared. Yet each turning she did the bare minimum, ensuring the new abode was liveable, then went off to enjoy her annual youth while it lasted.

In the garden, the leaves changed colours, swapped out their green for amber and yellow, ochre and sepia. Those so inclined fell and were carried off on the biting breeze. The sky, perpetually iron-grey at this point, was occasionally lightened by white clouds, however more often darkened to thunderous black. The vegetables and flowers had died, turned dry, and shrivelled. She didn't plant fruit trees anymore for she moved so often, and hated to watch them wither prematurely as they inevitably synched with her eternal, truncated rhythm. The small town of Ashdown had served her well, and she in turn had served it, bringing all the boons attendant upon the October Widow's tenure. The secret tithes she took seemed, to her, rather insignificant. The tiny offerings that staved off the moment when a larger one had to be made.

HENRY DID as he usually did and went straight around the back of the house, to the little shed where Mrs Morgan kept her hand-mower. He was late, but he knew the older woman wouldn't mind. 'As long as it's done by nightfall on Friday, Henry, I don't care what part of Friday you do it!' she'd said. But he liked to be reliable. He liked her to know that she could count on him. This morning his pickup had a punctured tyre; it looked as though a knife had been stuck into the tread, but he couldn't for the life of him figure out who would want to do him an ill turn. He'd taken his brother's battered VW instead of wasting time changing the flat.

He began where he always did: out the front, with its tiny patches of grass broken up by flower beds filled with dead plants; the rose bushes looked especially sad, bare but for their thorns and the crinkled brown remains of red and pink blooms. The mower was stubborn, though he'd oiled it only last week, and took more than a few enthusiastic shoves before the blades loosened and did their job. He hated the thing, but enjoyed the workout it gave. If it were but a bit warmer he'd have his hoodie and t-shirt off, so the three teenage girls who lived next door could peek out and watch him sweat and glisten in the afternoon sun. But that time was done, the season passed. Too cold now for such exhibitionism; he had to keep his peacock preening to the public bar in the evenings until next summer.

He moved into the back, which was the easier spot, the vegetable beds running along the side fences, out of the way, leaving the rest a clear run right up to the edge of the property where lawn met woods in a hard line. The garden did not gradually grow wild and blend into a creeping foliage that led to full-blown forest. Just ended in a stern demarcation line between the tame and the uncultivated. A creak and a tumbling sound snapped his head up to see three crows flapping and finding new perches; their previous branch had broken and hit the ground just as he looked. Black eyes regarded him curiously, somehow fondly. There must have been something dead in the undergrowth, he decided. Dead or dying. They were waiting until it was weak enough.

He reached the boundary and turned the recalcitrant machine. The curtains on the kitchen window twitched aside. Mrs Morgan stood at the sink, giving him a wide smile. She made the usual hand gestures: *Come inside when you're finished,*

I'll make you a hot drink. And there'd be buns too, freshly baked, warm enough to melt the butter and run the thick raspberry jam thin. She'd put a little whisky in his coffee: *Irish it up,* she'd say like she always did. And she'd smile and he'd smile back, watch her as she moved around the small kitchen, never still, but never hurried, always assured, seemingly always in the spot where she was meant to be.

And he'd watch how her hips swayed, how her breath made the breasts covered by her lilac blouse shift up and down, how shapely her calves were beneath the hem of the black skirt. How her face was shaped just like a sweetheart, her lips full, her skin creamy, her eyes not quite blue and not quite green but caught somewhere between. How any wrinkles were shallow and made by laughter not loss. How graceful her hands, her wrists, her fingers were as they reached towards him to lead him upstairs so he might see to Mirabel Morgan's other needs.

Cecil Davis, despite his grief and rage, had not become sloppy in anything but his personal hygiene. If the woman had gotten wind of his presence, she'd have fled, he was certain, no matter how invested she was in remaining in Ashdown. He'd tracked her for so long and, having found her, rented a house two doors down and on the opposite side of the street. It gave him an uninterrupted view of her property. He kept the curtains closed, but affixed cameras under the eaves, trained them on the woman's cottage. The place had come furnished, which was convenient, but hadn't mattered one way or the other to him. He'd have happily brought along the sleeping bag and air mattress he'd once used for camping and then, later still, for surveillance after . . .

He'd even managed to plant a GPS tracking device on her car, something impossible to notice unless you were actively looking for it. He didn't have to leave his four walls, just stared at the monitors he had rigged up so he could keep an eye on her comings and goings while he still managed to run his software support business from a separate laptop. The business he'd hoped to pass on now had as its sole purpose keeping the money coming in to fund his mission.

She's was going by Mrs Morgan, though his researches showed she recycled her names as she went, different ones each time, no discernible order, but he'd learned them, if not all then many. Knowing what to look for meant he had found her at last, though it took him seven years. Seven years of hacking utilities records, bank records, seeing patterns, recognising names, catching the scent. As much as anything it was his willingness to believe in strange things when no one else would.

It had taken all his determination, all the internal resources that had made him a successful businessman, to keep him focused. To keep him going after . . .

Of course, he could only watch the exterior of the house. He'd not gone into her home, couldn't bring himself to do that, though he'd never admit it was fear. *Caution*, for a fox will smell if anything else has been in its lair. *Caution*, he'd have said if there'd been anyone to talk to about it, if the police in Ottery St Mary's had listened with anything but pity, or the parents in the other small villages he'd gone to after ...

The young man who did the gardening was there again, in spite of the penknife Cecil had stuck in the back tyre of his vehicle, trying to put an obstacle in his way. Cecil had to admit, however, it hadn't been a very effective obstacle. Cecil was aware that if he approached the man, tried to tell him what he knew, he'd come across as a nutter, that the lad would back away, go straight to the woman, and warn her. Though he'd let things like bathing and general grooming fall by the wayside, Cecil knew there were some illusions he needed to keep intact.

He'd do what he could to protect the lad, within reason. He was someone's son after all, and Cecil had no wish for another father, another mother, to go through what he had; to wake and find their boy gone forever, become no more than motes of dust on the wind. He blinked as thoughts of Gil, tall and strong, young and vital, made heated tears rise, made the tendons of his heart thrum deep and discordant.

Cecil looked away from the screens, to the corner of the sitting room, where his gear lay in a pile. He still wasn't sure what to take with him. He knew where she would be, where she'd been going these past weeks, the place she had been preparing. But he didn't know what to take, what would work. He didn't really know *what* she was.

He only knew that when he confronted her there would be no words, no recriminations, no time-wasting that might give her a moment's chance to escape. He doubted she remembered Gil. He doubted she remembered any, certainly not by name. He suspected there had been so many she couldn't keep track of them all.

No. No words. Whatever he might say didn't matter. Wouldn't matter. It was only what he *did* tomorrow evening that mattered.

SHE LAY BACK, listening to Henry's heavy footsteps retreating down the stairs, the rattling of the pipes as he ran a shower. The smell of him was strong in her nostrils, the sweat from manual labour ever an aphrodisiac. He'd been worried, when they first started this, that she'd become pregnant. She'd laughed so hard at the idea that he'd been offended, thought she was impugning his fertility, his gods-given right to get her up the duff. He'd required stroking, reassuring, promises that it wasn't him but *her*. In their months together he'd had no more cause for complaint; his time might be brief but she gave him the best of herself, helped him live full. He got what he wanted and she took pleasure in it too, taught him a few things that had made his eyes grow round. Taught him a few more things she didn't mind if he tried out on others, younger women. She was not jealous, did not need his singular adoration, considered her lessons a gift. *You're welcome.*

The mattress beneath her was soft and she gave it a fond pat. A fine thing that had done good service. She wasn't always so lucky when she rented a new house: fully furnished was essential for her lifestyle. Having to pick up and pack everything once a year was a burden she'd long ago dispensed with. Only ever own what you can't do without. Only ever have essential things that you can fit in a single small bag. Travel lightly, live deeply, serve faithfully.

And she had done that. Done it for so long she could barely remember when she hadn't been what she'd become. What she was. Could barely remember a time before that first fire, that first night, before she took the mantle from the one before her. She saw no time in front of her either, when she might relinquish the position. It was her duty, her obligation, her keeping of the faith. She would not let it go easily. Besides, where might she find someone to replace her?

Sometimes it was hard, she admitted, to maintain such single-minded devotion when the world around her changed quickly, quickly. Much more so than before. Difficult to be a fixed point in a whirling universe, holding to an idea, a certainty, an allegiance, a moral obligation. She took some comfort when the core of things stayed true: soul cakes had become candy, but the idea of *benefaction* was still there.

And the fires.

The fires were always lit.

The fires remained.

And the sacrifices could still be made, though the ideas underpinning them drew cries and condemnations in this soft society. Still they were needful things, if only people appreciated that something had to be given back in order for the wheel to spin, for the earth to bloom anew. A child lost here, a pet taken there—the tiny sacrifices that kept the world going until the larger giving might happen.

She did not like to take small girls, little cauldrons of life that they were, so much potential lost when their flame guttered. An unhelpful sacrifice that almost lost more than it gained. But the wee boys … Ah, the boys were like tadpoles, only good for Mischief Night pranks, and so many of them spawned … How could one or three be missed? How could they be seen as anything but small coin in return for the greatest gift?

But no one thought like her anymore. Or no one worthwhile. Murderers, cultists, wasters, and nihilists, who neither knew nor cared what they did. Whose killings and leavings brought no benefit, just the brief satisfaction of destruction for the individual.

No, no one thought like her anymore. That was why she'd had to prepare the glade on the wooded tor herself, prepare the fire alone; there were no acolytes nowadays, no pretty maids to do the grunt work; her only handmaidens were black and feathered, sharp-eyed and beaked. She grinned. Just her, lugging branches, oak and larch and yew, collecting the smaller tinder, and constructing it all into something that resembled a bed, a bier, a pyre. Threading it with mistletoe, mandrake, mugwort and rue. Doing what was required for when the doors between life and un-life opened and the dead danced through, to visit loved ones or to exact vengeance on rivals and enemies.

Downstairs the closing of the front door sounded. Henry

was gone. Strangely, she felt bereft. She rolled onto her side, curled into a ball, and closed her eyes, slowed her breathing, commanding her body to sleep deep and late. Soon the changes would come and she would need all her energy for the next night.

THE DAY BEGAN DEATHLY grey and did not improve. The afternoon light into which Henry stepped was so weak and ineffectual that he almost missed the crouched man. If he'd not been heading towards the pickup he'd spent part of the morning changing the tyre of, he'd not have seen the man at all. As he got closer Henry saw the dull gleam of a blade, not terribly big, but big enough to do damage. The man was about to puncture the tyre yet again.

A red veil covered Henry's eyes. His temper wasn't short, not by a long shot, but nor was he inclined to forgive this kind of spiteful vandalism. He didn't know who the bloke was or why he was targeting Henry, and at that point he didn't care. The youth took swift steps, got close enough for the other to hear him and begin to turn and rise.

Henry threw himself forward.

Henry stopped.

The rank body odour hit him first, then the man's fist punched him in the stomach. Henry caught a glimpse of a frightened weary face, rumpled as if someone had slept in it too long, mud-green eyes swimming in fear and guilt, and a mouth that kept saying something over and over. Henry's hearing had deserted him, the world fallen silent, and his belly flared both hot and cold.

He looked down.

The knife was protruding from his hard-earned six-pack.

He didn't think the man had meant to do it; it was just the angle, Henry's momentum, the man's fright. He wanted to say, *It's okay*, that he knew it hadn't been on purpose. Noise began to seep back to him, and he heard the man yelling *Help! Help!* as he caught at Henry and laid him down on the footpath. *Help! Help!* as he ran away so he wouldn't get caught. As if he had something better to do.

Chills rushed through him, up and down. Henry hoped someone would let Mrs Morgan know he wouldn't make it tonight. He hoped he wouldn't feel worse. He hoped someone would come soon.

CECIL RAN like he'd never done before. He wasn't a runner. He was a short, fat, middle-aged man burdened by grief and junk food. After Gil had gone, after Cecil's wife had left him, no one cared for him, not even Cecil. He just kept going, knowing he needed nourishment and nothing more. He didn't eat for taste or enjoyment or health, but just to exist. It meant he wasn't fussy with portions or calories; it meant things fried deeply and provided quickly formed a major part of his diet. He couldn't remember the last time he'd eaten a piece of fruit, or there'd been something in his fridge that was green because it was meant to be, rather than green because it was going off—and Cecil's refrigerator was the place things went to die. He ran, though he knew he couldn't be as fast as he felt, as if things sped by in the grey dusk. As if he flew along the deserted streets as he fled the terrible mistake he'd made.

He'd stopped shouting soon after he'd let the boy down, pressing the lad's large hands to the wound. He'd pulled out the knife, knowing it would make the lad bleed all the worse, but Cecil couldn't leave it behind. There were his prints—a drunk-driving conviction fifteen years ago meant he'd be on file—and he didn't want to let the thing go because it had been Gil's. He hoped someone had gone to the boy's aid, hoped it wasn't the sort of neighbourhood where shouting caused people to secure their doors and huddle inside until everything seemed quiet again. But he couldn't stay. He couldn't get caught. He was so close.

He stumbled over the threshold of his rented house and slammed the door, pressed his forehead against it, then turned, rested his back on the wood, waited until the breath shooting from his lungs didn't feel like fire, until the shaking of his limbs had calmed. And then he bent over and vomited hard on the tenant-resistant, slate-coloured carpet. He huddled, hands wrapped around his head, ragged nails biting through his thinning hair into the pale scalp beneath.

The pain brought him back to himself.

He had to focus.

He had to go on.

This was his chance.

He couldn't let it—her—slip away again.

He forced himself upwards. He had hours yet; he should clean the mess he'd made, watch the monitors. But somehow he knew he couldn't wait them out here. He should go. He should go before the streets began to hold traces of random trick-or-treaters. What if someone had seen? What if he'd left some trace, though he couldn't image what it might be. What if, what if, what if? What if the police were already speeding towards this place?

The thought galvanised him. He picked through the gear in the sitting room, extracted the sleeping bag for warmth and the ghillie suit for camouflage. In the end he took only the Swiss Army knife, wiping its blade as clean as he could, stuffing it in a trouser pocket.

He knew where she would go.

He knew where he would meet her.

• • •

THE AIR WAS BRISK, lacing her lungs as she breathed deeply, taking long strides up the incline. Once she'd have carried a burning brand to illuminate her track, to ignite the pyre, but that might have caught attention. So, it was a Maglite in her hand, providing a bright circle to follow, but giving off no warmth the way an old torch would. It was enough that the *form* of things be honoured in spirit, not slavish mimicry.

Around her, foxes yipped and badgers snuffled. Other things she couldn't identify made noise too, but Mirabel had no fear of the dark, no fear of the forest. She'd walked across the fields then taken the path around the base of the tor, traversing rills and ditches, stiles and fallen trees, marking the way with light, the way that must lead ever upwards. When she passed under the canopy of trees that would take her to the glade, where Henry would be waiting, she sighed contentedly. In her long years, she had never been let down by any of her chosen. All things had their time, their natural conclusion.

Everything she directed her existence towards was coming to fruition.

CECIL ALMOST GASPED as she moved past him in the darkness. Her face was shadowed, but he knew it was her, knew her shape; he'd watched her enough from the first time they'd met. From when she'd moved in across the street from his family home in Ottery St Mary and lived there for a year. The lovely, gracious woman who'd asked politely if their son, their only child, just turned nineteen, might be kind enough to do some gardening for her. Effortlessly attractive, effortlessly desirable.

The woman who'd come and gone like a storm, like a flood, stealing something so precious he'd not cared to see what she'd left behind, the benefits she'd given to a village that had been foundering, its crops poor and stunted, its children pale and sickly, its businesses and farms dying a slow death. A village that, after Gil had gone, began to breathe, to produce, to be *fertile* again, though that benevolence gladdened Cecil's heart not a jot.

She walked slowly, he noticed, slower than seemed normal. He wondered if she'd injured herself crossing dark fields, then reminded himself it didn't matter. He waited until she was well ahead, then rolled from the sleeping bag, left it and the ghillie suit behind, and began to follow.

She reached the top of the slope, stepped into the clearing. The bulk of the woven bed was there, picked out by the beam of the Maglite. On top lay the torch she she'd made, a branch of yew, one end wrapped around with dried henbane and belladonna and other lesser kindling. She lit it with the matches in her coat pocket and switched off the flashlight. The burning brand gave better light and she nodded with satisfaction, feeling her blood warmed by the leaping blue-orange flame. She held it high and looked around.

No sign of Henry.

She frowned.

Called his name and received no reply.

Looked at the cheap watch on her wrist, even though she didn't need to, the tides in her veins kept track of the hours. Fifteen minutes. He still had fifteen minutes.

She threw the brand onto the pyre; that at least could be started. She felt the heat and smiled, welcoming it like an old friend to warm her ancient bones.

Once the blaze was settled, she turned her back to it as she always did, knowing the bright amber light made of her a silhouette so Henry, as he came up the bridal path, could not see the change in her. Could not see how, on Halloween Eve, age had rushed in upon her, how all the seasons' endings had converged where she stood, rendering her old, weakened, vulnerable.

Tension was beginning to take a hold on Mirabel when she at last saw the blurred shape appear at the mouth of the path; her eyes aged too, let her down. A man, yes. Henry, she thought, and relaxed into a smile. He wouldn't see her face, not until the last moment, and by then it wouldn't matter.

She raised her hands, stretched out her arms to welcome him, though it caused an ache in her hoary joints, a popping she feared was audible. Her smile would not be dimmed, however, as she felt the ebbing that was essential for a new beginning.

Henry came towards her, faster now, faster, and as he got closer she knew something was wrong.

HER FACE WAS A BLANK, black oval to Cecil, his eyes burned by the glare of the bonfire behind her, but he saw in the way she shifted that she *knew*. She knew somehow.

That something was not right.

And Cecil was filled with an unreasoning terror that she would get away. That she would turn into a puff of smoke, sprout wings and fly, become airy in the extreme, and sink into the earth's arms, away from his. He put on a burst of speed, the last he'd ever make, propelling his fat little self forward until his soft body met her bony one, and he heard bones break with the impact, heard her gasp turn into a shriek as they both plummeted back, against the pyre, then into its heart as flames reached up and around to envelop them.

And in that moment, that final moment, Cecil experienced with startling clarity a rare self-awareness. He knew, at last, that his question for the October Widow was not and had never been *Why my son?* but rather *Why not me?*

WHEN SHE WOKE she sensed an earth changed and not for the better. She sensed that she had changed, also not for the better. She ached, not as badly as on her last night, but still a dull throb of pain ran through her. Where was the spring in her step, the strength in her form that renewal had always promised and ever delivered?

The October Widow had slept for two solid days in the ashes and bones, the dirt and cinders, while the land and her body reknitted themselves, made themselves anew, the debt called in with the blood of the young king.

She shook her head. Her memories were loose, scrambled, rattling around in her head as though her skull were too big for her brain. Lying back in her cold charcoal bed, Mirabel closed her eyes, breathed deep, trying to centre herself, to pull the core together.

No. Not the young king. Not her consort, *not* her sacrifice.

Someone else. A man, yes, but not Henry. A man, older, soft and lost, barely holding on to his life. A man weak and whimpering, clasping her as if she were a mother who'd failed to love him.

A man who didn't know what he'd done.

Slowly, she raised her hands, examined them. Brown-spotted, dry, fingers twigs, nails broken and brittle, joints swollen. She put them to her face and felt the damage there: skin corrugated, furrowed like a field before planting. The eyebrows bushy, the dips beneath the eyes so soft they felt like decayed fruit, and the chin—oh, the chin! Raised lumps ... not moles, nothing so benign, but *warts*. With stiff sharp hairs growing from them.

Slowly she rolled to one side, drew her legs towards her

chest, then rolled onto hands and knees, as if to search for something in the cinders, as if to beg. When at last she found her feet, she dug them through the clinkers and soot, ignoring the sharp bits of broken, unconsumed bone, until she found the ground proper. Looked down at her naked body as she waited, saw firsthand the damage done by an inappropriate forfeit: stretch-marked skin, empty dugs for breast, scrawny arms, a hollow pelvis, thighs destined never to meet, knees like knucklebones, calves no more than long ankles. The October Widow shuddered. She closed her eyes again, concentrated. Listened. Felt.

She'd always known where to travel next, for the pulse of the world directed her. But now … Now it was weak, so weak she could barely feel it beneath the soles of her feet. She had to kneel once more, press her ear and her palms to the dirt, heedless of the grey-black that coated her flesh, to try and find it. To hear its voice more clearly.

She straightened. There was a message, yes, but it wasn't a location, not yet. The world wasn't strong enough to know, for everywhere the slow decline that a lesser offering brought was beginning. That man, she thought, that stupid sad little man had dumped all his grieving, all his pain into the sacred fire, into her, into the earth. Left his mark behind and it would not be easily erased.

But it *could* be done.

She *would* do it.

In that renewal would be her own, the little man's stain washed away with a tide of young blood.

Only the Dead and the Moonstruck

JESSE BULLINGTON EMAILED to say he was putting together an anthology called *Letters to Lovecraft*, in which all the stories would take their inspiration from Lovecraft's famous essay 'Supernatural Horror in Literature'. I think I'd only ever written one Lovecraftian story before, that being 'Rising, Not Dreaming' for Silvia Moreno-Garcia's Innsmouth Free Press. I was apprehensive but game. I read the essay, picked out the line that starts "Children will always be afraid of the dark", and carried on from there. I had the picture in my head of a very domestic scene, a family broken by loss, the protagonist Becky so very young and trying to keep her remaining family together—and also wracked by guilt. The story also became a kind of exercise in the old adage about being careful what you wish for.

Cuckoo

I wrote this story when Steve Jones asked me for something for *A Book of Horrors*—it needed to be more proper horror than I normally wrote, he insisted. So, I wrote this tale about a vengeance demon trying very hard to do its job ... but encountering something even it couldn't bear. Sidenote: Steve rejected it! Said I could do better. He was right: I wrote 'The Coffin-Maker's Daughter' for him, and it won a British Fantasy Award. 'Cuckoo' found a home in *A Killer Among Demons*.

The Burning Circus

The delightful Johnny Mains asked if I'd write something for one of his British Fantasy Society anthologies, so I did. I had the title and the name Semiramis (an ancient Armenian queen/goddess), and the image of a woman walking unevenly because only one of her shoes had a heel. I kept thinking of this pair of feet wandering along through different landscapes, always off-beat, the rhythm strangely broken, kicking up dust and small pebbles; eventually I figured out that she'd been punished unjustly, and was determined to seek revenge. Queen Semiramis had a connection with the doves of Ishtar, and this gave me my weapon of vengeance.

Home and Hearth

Spectral Press asked for a ghost story for their chapbook collection in 2013. I've always wondered about parents whose children kill: those who go to any lengths to protect their little monster, and those who decide they're responsible for protecting the world. I wondered what it must do to your sense of self. 'Home and Hearth' is my way of wondering through a version of that trauma.

Winter Children

Nick Gevers of PS asked for a story back in 2011. I was still processing the death of my maternal grandmother and had a lot of grief I didn't know what to do with—so I turned it into a story. I'd hoped that it would be something inspiring and uplifting, something that reflected the sort of person she was. What I got instead was 'Winter Children', in which children are easily lost and bad things hide in unlikely places. Sorry, Grandma!

Pale Tree House

This bit of very short fiction was written for a charity anthology a long while ago. I wanted to do a tribute to M. R. James, that echoed the kinds of ghost stories he told. It's got a lot of 'Lost Hearts' at its core.

The Red Forest

This is the only previously unpublished story in this collection. I had a series of images in my head that eventually settled into a tale: a girl watching from windows, the ghost of an old man tending pigeons in a ruined Russian church, and blood dripping from trees. Oh, and Baba Yaga offering deals to desperate people. A big thank-you to Haralambi Markov for his perceptive critique!

The Song of Sighs

Another story I wrote for Steve Jones, who requested a kind of Cthulhu fairy tale for *Weirder Shadows Over Innsmouth*. When I started thinking about it, I ended up with a Cthulhu biblical fairy tale: modelled the verses at the start of each section on 'The Song of Solomon', added a princess with a lost memory, a dash of the Gothic, and a school for orphans. Not really the best reading before bedtime.

The Dead Ones Don't Hurt You

My first zombie outing, which I wrote for Clarion South in 2009. It has been considerably reworked: from a smarmy short it has evolved into something much darker. It sprang out of my vague annoyance with people (generally women) who are so desperate for relationships that they'll put up with anything in order to keep a partner; I then married this with the tradition of zombies not as Romero's supercharged-brain-eating monsters, but as slaves. I wanted to hark back to proper zombie lore, with the creatures as compliant servants who'll return to their graves if fed salt.

Sun Falls

Ticonderoga Publications wanted a vampire story for *Dead Red Heart* in 2011. Initially I wasn't going to submit, as I had no vampire stories in mind and didn't want to join the red river of writers working on bloodsucker tales. Then I got the image of Terry in my head, driving a muscle car away from a destroyed city landscape, tapping her finger on the wheel, and with her vampire boss's head in an Esky on the backseat. You can't resist that.

The Way of All Flesh

I'd written this story with no market in mind; it was just there with Sweet Bobby Tate and Annabel Adams moving towards each other on a collision course in Wolf's Briar. Bobby's tone is kind of how I imagine Alan Moore's A. A. Rouse sounds in 'I Travel in Suspenders' (*Voice of the Fire*). It's kind of a zombie story without the zombies, first published in *Suspended in Dusk*.

The October Widow

Mark Morris asked for a story for his first *Spectral Book of Horror Stories*. I'd had the title floating around in my head for a long while, but no story to go with it. Then I got the main character's name, then I could see the house she lived in, but I knew she was always transient, only staying there for a short time. I knew she was doing something important and that a foolish man was going to interrupt that.

Previous Publication Credits

'Only the Dead and the Moonstruck' was first published in *Letters to Lovecraft* (Jesse Burlington, ed.), Stone Skin Press, 2014.

'Cuckoo' was first published in *A Killer Among Demons* (Craig Bezant, ed.), Dark Prints Press, 2013.

'The Burning Circus' was first published in *The Burning Circus* (Johnny Mains, ed.), British Fantasy Society, 2013.

'Home and Hearth' was first published in *The Spectral Press Chapbook Series* (Simon Marshall-Jones, ed.), Spectral Press, 2014.

'Winter Children' was first published in *Postscripts 32/33: Far Voyager* (Nick Gevers and Peter Crowther, eds.), PS Publishing, 2014.

'Pale Tree House' was first published in *100 Lightnings*, Paroxysm Press, April 2016.

'The Red Forest' is a new story, published here for the first time.

'The Song of Sighs' was first published in *Weirder Shadows Over Innsmouth* (Stephen Jones, ed.), Fedogan and Bremer, 2013.

'The Dead Ones Don't Hurt You' was first published in *The Girl with No Hands and Other Tales*, Ticonderoga Publications, 2010.

'Sun Falls' was first published in *Dear Red Heart* (Russell B. Farr, ed.), Ticonderoga Publications, 2011.

'The Way of All Flesh' was first published in *Suspended in Dusk* (Simon Dewar, ed.), Books of the Dead Press, 2014.

'The October Widow' was first published in *The Spectral Book of Horror: Volume One* (Mark Morris, ed.), Spectral Press, 2014.

Angela Slatter is the author of the supernatural crime novels *Vigil*, *Corpselight* and *Restoration* from Jo Fletcher Books, as well as nine short story collections, including *The Girl with No Hands and Other Tales*, *Sourdough and Other Stories*, *The Bitterwood Bible and Other Recountings*, and *A Feast of Sorrows: Stories*. She is also the author of the novellas, *Of Sorrow and Such* and *Ripper*.

Vigil was nominated for the Dublin Literary Award in 2018, and Angela has won a World Fantasy Award, a British Fantasy Award, a Ditmar, an Australian Shadows Award and six Aurealis Awards. She has recently signed a two-book deal with Titan Books for *All The Murmuring Bones* and *Morwood*, gothic fantasies set in the world of the *Sourdough* and *Bitterwood* collections.

Angela's short stories have appeared in Australian, UK and US *Best Of* anthologies such *The Mammoth Book of New Horror, The Year's Best Dark Fantasy and Horror, The Best Horror of the Year, The Year's Best Australian Fantasy and Horror, and The Year's Best YA Speculative Fiction*. Her work has been translated into Bulgarian, Chinese, Russian, Italian, Spanish, Japanese, Polish, French and Romanian. Victoria Madden of Sweet Potato Films (*The Kettering Incident*) has optioned the film rights to one of her short stories ("Finnegan's Field").

She has an MA and a PhD in Creative Writing, is a graduate of Clarion South 2009 and the Tin House Summer Writers Workshop 2006, and in 2013 she was awarded one of the inaugural Queensland Writers Fellowships. In 2016 Angela was the Established Writer-in-Residence at the Katharine Susannah Prichard Writers Centre in Perth. She has been awarded career development funding by Arts Queensland, the Copyright Agency and, in 2017/18, an Australia Council for the Arts grant.

Find her online at www.angelaslatter.com

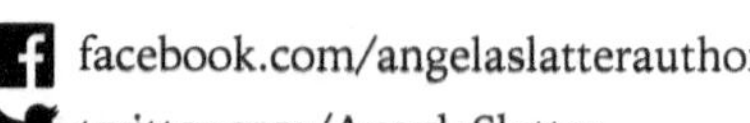
facebook.com/angelaslatterauthor
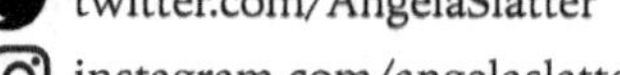
twitter.com/AngelaSlatter
instagram.com/angelaslatter

Thank You For Buying This Brain Jar Press
Chapbook

To receive special offers, bonus content, and info on
new releases and other great reads, visit us
online at www.BrainJarPress.com